David Amey was born in Swindon and moved to Dorset as a child, where he still lives with his wife and four children.

Having always had a passion for all things horror, and a love for the paranormal, David decided to push the boundaries of what he considers a genre that is neglected and being left behind. He brings a new type of horror to his readers; one that pokes their imagination like a hornet's nest and brings a real fear to the written word.

You will be pulled in by anything he writes, but beware, there is no escape from his dark mind.

This one is for you, Mum. Thanks for believing in me and not letting me give up. All your encouragement has been both eye rolling and ear bending at times, but fantastic nonetheless. Henry would never have been heard and let loose if not for you.

For Dad, you taught me the true power of the written word and showed me what it could do. I miss you, but I know you're always near.

And, for Kirsty, Samantha, James, Poppy and Ryan.

David Amey

Splitting Man

AUSTIN MACAULEY PUBLISHERS™

LONDON * CAMBRIDGE * NEW YORK * SHARJAH

Copyright © David Amey 2022

The right of David Amey to be identified as author of this work has been asserted by the author in accordance with section 77 and 78 of the Copyright, Designs and Patents Act 1988.

All rights reserved. No part of this publication may be reproduced, stored in a retrieval system, or transmitted in any form or by any means, electronic, mechanical, photocopying, recording, or otherwise, without the prior permission of the publishers.

Any person who commits any unauthorised act in relation to this publication may be liable to criminal prosecution and civil claims for damages.

This is a work of fiction. Names, characters, businesses, places, events, locales, and incidents are either the products of the author's imagination or used in a fictitious manner. Any resemblance to actual persons, living or dead, or actual events is purely coincidental.

A CIP catalogue record for this title is available from the British Library.

ISBN 9781398413085 (Paperback)
ISBN 9781398413092 (ePub e-book)

www.austinmacauley.com

First Published 2022
Austin Macauley Publishers Ltd®
1 Canada Square
Canary Wharf
London
E14 5AA

My thanks and appreciation to all of you out there who have helped and encouraged me in the writing of this book. Thanks for all the bent ears I gave you, and the wonderful advice you gave to me.

Thanks to Gary, my best friend, for allowing me to put him within my pages once again.

Thanks to Toby and Kit, two great guys who not only supplied me with the best coffee ever, but also let me use them within the book.

Thanks to Terence Byford, a fantastic author who acted as my personal bottle of Tip-Ex.

A special thanks to Claire Smith. Thank you for taking a chance and believing in me. Your support will not be forgotten. And of course, Steve Smith, with his unique idea and interpretation of what the word 'support' means.

Austin Macauley Publishers, the team that have built this book into what you now hold, thank you.

And of course, Henry, who told me his story first.

If I have missed anyone, I apologise to you and thank you now.

Of course, the biggest thanks go to you, the reader. Thank you so much for buying this book. I hope you enjoy it and will continue to read my words.

Chapter 1
1749 - Henry

"Henry. Henry, what do you think you are doing, you doddering halfwit? This mess of yours needs tidying up, and I do mean now. Our guests shall be arriving soon and I will not stand to have your disgusting lumbering presence here when they do."

Lady Castleleigh shouted at her wood splitter, he was a slow-witted, but hardworking gentle giant of a man. Henry stopped what he was doing; he dropped the log that he was holding in his hand and looked up at the lady as she stood before him with her hands placed on her hips. She was, in his slow mind, a very pretty lady. He could, of course, never tell her that, so he smiled his lopsided, gap-toothed smile at her. Henry remembered that he must not speak unless the lord had first commanded it of him. To speak any words to the lady would be to invite another brutal beating upon himself at the hands of Lord Castleleigh.

Henry thought back to a couple of days before, when the lord and lady's daughter, young Molly, had sat watching him as he split logs with his great wood axe. He liked little Molly, she was kind to him and she would teach him nursery rhymes and they would sing together as he went about his work and split his wood. They were still singing a song that Molly had just finished teaching Henry, a new happy song when his lordship appeared.

The sudden silence in the grounds was almost deafening when he had seen the lord standing there glaring at him then he turned to his daughter and quietly asked Molly to wait inside for him whilst he had a little private talk with Henry. Whilst Molly disappeared, he had walked up to Henry and grabbing a huge handful of his hair and raised his head. He looked up in utter revulsion at Henry's face.

"Listen to me very carefully, Henry," he said quietly, almost a whisper so that Henry had to strain to hear what his lord was saying to him. "I will tell you this but the once, you great buffoon, I have had a gut full of you damn log splitters. The whole lot of you are nothing but dark curses upon my family, you bring nothing with you but trouble. You will stay far away from my daughter and you will stay even further away from my lady wife. You will never open that big stupid mouth of yours again unless I command it first. You are less than worthless, you ignorant oaf. I do not give you the coin to fraternise with my family; you are here for the sole purpose of splitting logs for my home fires and no more. Now bow your big stupid ugly head and take your punishment well, learn this lesson fast. I will not ever repeat myself again."

Henry bowed his great head as Lord Castleleigh released him and reached down for one of the logs that Henry had been splitting; grasping the wood with two hands, he swung it down with all of his strength on the back of Henry's head. Henry began to cry as his legs buckled and gave way beneath him; the lord laughed loudly as he continued hitting him over and over with the log. He beat every visible part of Henry's body, his arms, legs, back, chest and head.

When he had finished, Henry hurt everywhere. Although he could not see anything through all the blood that had leaked into his eyes, he knew that his face was a mess; he could only see in a blurry red haze out of one eye because the other had swollen shut. He could not speak through all the bloody and puffy lips. Henry had learnt his lesson and would not ever speak out of turn again.

The lord walked away, dropping the bloody and splintered log as he went. "Do not ever forget our little talk, Henry." Henry hung his head and cried.

Henry looked down at Lady Castleleigh through his one good eye, grinning madly at her. He waited for her to speak again.

"We are having guests later, Henry, I want the main hall to be well stacked with logs to keep us all warm this evening. As for this mess, I will not tell you again. Clear it away or Lord Castleleigh will know about it. Do you think you can manage to understand and carry out my instructions, you great idiot of a man? Can you manage it or do I need to make my instructions even clearer so that they will sink into whatever it is that you have wedged between your big fat ears," she said with contempt, throwing a hateful glare at the huge ugly man standing quietly in front of her.

"Uh huh," Henry managed to mutter through his still swollen and split lips. He tried to smile friendly at the lady.

"What do you think you are smiling at, you great oaf? Look at the stinking state of you. Why, you're not even a bad pale shadow of Edward. You cannot even talk like a real man, can you? Now, I mean it, I want you to—"

Lady Castleleigh did not finish her sentence; she was so busy belittling Henry that she did not notice where she was treading. As she walked around him, she tripped over his pile of split logs. There was a great dull squelch as she fell and landed face first on Henry's upturned wood axe.

Henry could only stare as the ground around the lady's head began to darken with her spilt blood, her body began to convulse and twitch madly. Finally, she just lay still and unmoving with her face burying the axe head deep.

Panicking, Henry rushed to her side and fell to his knees beside the lady and roughly put his hands on her so that he could turn her over. The soft of Lady Castleleigh's face could not support the heavy weight of his axe, so as she was turned over, the axe fell away from her ruined face, taking her nose, cheek and an eye with it as it fell, red, to the sodden ground beside her.

Henry did not know what to do, but he was sure that the lord will be so very angry with him if he did nothing. He knew Lord Castleleigh would know exactly what to do. Hastily, he picked up her limp body in his huge arms and put her across his wide shoulders. He could feel the blood escaping from her ruined face as it cascaded down his neck and chest. Henry stopped to pick up his axe. He did not want for some other to have an accident as well. If he did not take it and some other got hurt, maybe even little Molly, he would for sure be blamed and severely beaten. He hastened for the house and his lord. They left a thin trail of blood behind them as Henry, with his lady bouncing along on his shoulders, made their way up to the house.

Henry had just started to climb the stone steps up to the entrance foyer when the front doors burst open and out came a bounding little blond girl. Molly was not looking where she was running and collided at full speed with Henry; she bounced off him and landed hard and unceremoniously on her backside, staring up in wonder at the man mountain she had just run into. Slowly, her gaze rose up his body until she saw what no child should ever see, her own mother's bloody body draped across the vast shoulders of Henry. Molly watched in shock as a small drop of blood fell from her mother's ruined face and landed on her cheek. Molly opened her mouth and screamed at the top of her lungs in sheer terror.

Henry panicked at the noise and carelessly dropped Lady Castleleigh's body to the ground and made to grab Molly by the arm so that he may try and comfort her. She saw her mother fall to the floor and she saw the bloody axe in the giant's hand as he grabbed her. She didn't understand what was happening. It should not have been possible but a terrified Molly screamed louder and louder.

Henry was really scared by her screams, what was wrong with his little best friend Molly? He held on to her, gripping tighter as he started to back uncertainly away. He didn't mean too. In fact, he didn't even realise that he was, but he started to drag the terrified Molly along in his blind panic. He stumbled over the body, pulling Molly over it as well, covering the poor girl in her own mother's blood.

"Let her go, Henry."

Henry spun around fast, scared to death at the sound of the booming voice. He let go of Molly's arm and forgot all about the axe as well, letting it fall to the floor as he found himself staring down the long barrel of Lord Castleleigh's hunting rifle.

Henry instinctively began to raise his hands in fear as he stumbled backwards and away from the threatening rifle in his lord's hands. Henry did not hear the sound as the gun discharged and he didn't feel the pain as the shot tore through his knee. All he knew was that his leg would no longer work and wouldn't support his weight as he crashed down first on to one knee and then he fell backwards to the ground.

Henry looked down his body in confusion and horror at his leg and the red ruin that was once his kneecap; his leg was bent but try as hard as he could, he found that he could not straighten it. Blood began to pool around his leg. He was losing lots of blood and fast. He didn't understand why this was happening to him, why was Molly so scared of him all of a sudden? Why had his lordship attacked him with the rifle? He had to get away. Maybe if he could, then things would somehow be alright again. Terrified as he was, Henry managed to clumsily turn himself over onto his stomach. He had to get away. He started clawing desperately at the ground in front of him as he tried to crawl away, using his huge hands to pull his own body along the ground, trailing his now useless leg behind him.

A huge dark shadow fell across the ground around Henry's head. Henry looked, twisting his neck to see that Lord Castleleigh has discarded his rifle. A glint of sun on metal made Henry see his own wood axe in his lord's hand. Henry began to cry, he clawed urgently at the ground in an effort to get away. *Why is this happening?* he thought. *It was an accident and I was only been trying to help my lady. Why are they doing this to me? I not been bad. I only try to help.*

The axe head blurred passed Henry's face. He still tried to crawl but fell. As he looked forward, he saw his hand where he had left it. It was limp, unmoving and covered in blood, his blood. Henry lifted his arm and received a face full of his own blood as he looked on at the spurting stump, still he could feel no pain.

Thunk.

Henry lifted his second arm and stared in utter disbelief at his second spurting stump. Blood was flying everywhere and Henry was becoming numb all over. He was cold and shivering and getting colder by the second. He felt weak, weaker than he had ever felt in his life and he was scared. Tears and mucus mingled with the blood on his face as he cried like a little lost child; no longer possessing the strength needed to support himself, Henry collapsed.

There was a growing pressure on his side that he could feel, but in his distress, he paid it no heed until he found himself turning over and flopped onto his back, his head hitting the ground hard. Henry felt a very heavy and sudden, sharp pressure upon his chest. This time, he did pay attention. He managed with great effort, his teeth clenched in his struggle, to slowly lift his head up and look down his body. Henry could only gasp as he saw his own wood axe. Its large head was embedded deep in his chest. His mouth agape, Henry cast his eyes questioningly up at his lord's face.

"Rot in hell, you filthy animal, I should never have employed a soft bastard like you." Lord Castleleigh spat in his face. "I will need yet another new splitting man now, damn you."

Henry closed his eyes for the final time and saw no more as a last solitary tear slid slowly from the corner of his good eye and rolled down his cheek towards his ear.

The lord glanced at Molly. "Child, get inside. Get inside the house this instant."

Molly tearfully climbed the stone steps, rubbing at her sore arm where Henry had grabbed hold of her and she entered the house silently as he turned alone to face his wife's ruined body.

"You did this. You brought this on us all," he spoke gently to her. "I found your journal and I know what filthy disgusting acts you committed with our last splitter and what fruit came forth from that whoring, you damned disgusting woman. Maybe now you can go to him in his cold unmarked grave behind the stable and warm each other."

Taking one last look as his wife's destroyed beauty, he spat on her still warm body and walked solemnly away from her.

Chapter 2
1750 – Lord Castleleigh

"Molly, come, your supper is ready. Molly."

Lord Castleleigh impatiently walked through the door to the drawing room to see his wife's daughter sitting on the hard floor laughing at and talking to thin air.

He stood watching the young girl, a girl of six years, a beautiful girl who looked every bit just like her mother had. A little girl, who up until just a little over eighteen months ago, he had loved dearly and called his precious daughter. Now all he would or indeed could call her was either Molly or child; the lord could not look at her anymore without seeing her mother.

He had been sorting through some items in his bedchamber when he had, by pure chance, come across his wife's journal sat in a bottom drawer of her bureau. Picking it up curiously, he had crossed the room, sat on the edge of his bed and opened the journal. He began looking through the pages, confused at first, but slowly the confusion on his face turned to hurt and then to anger as his face reddened and he read on.

October 17

My lord husband employed a new log splitter today after the death of old Angus. Edward his name is. He is young and strong and quite handsome. He will, I am certain, make a fine addition to our staff.

I am taking the maid off to the market today, where we hope to purchase some fine meat for my dear lord husband's birthday next week.

Lord Castleleigh continued reading the journal. Some of the entries were of little or no importance to him and just a foolish woman's words. Certain entries however did happen to catch his eye and those words he read most carefully.

October 20

I stood at the open window of my bedchamber, watching earlier as Edward peeled off his heavy work shirt and began to split logs. Oh, what a joy it is to watch his sweating muscular body move as he works. He must be quite unhinged to strip on so cold a day as this. It did however make me feel quite warm and excited to watch him.

October 22

It is my lord husband's birthday tomorrow. I know that I should be so excited for him but I cannot help but think of Edward hard at work yesterday. I took it upon myself and had ventured out earlier to the log shed to fetch some choice logs for my lord husband's fire. I had intended on warming his study so that he would be comfortable upon his return.

As I entered the shed, I found Edward; he was stacking freshly split logs in the corner. He courteously helped me carry the heavy logs indoors and he kindly showed me the best way to start the fire correctly. Edward is such a polite, knowledgeable and handsome young man. He took my hand and kissed it most tenderly as he left. I do not know what it means but his kiss lighted something warm and happy inside of me. I fear that I am developing the most irrational and unnatural feelings for the man.

October 23

My husband it seems has had a fine day today. He is drinking heavily now with his business associates. He did however berate me most severely earlier when he had opened his gifts. He told me that he wants not these useless bits of junk and trinkets, but a son and heir. He demanded to know when would I bless him and become with child. I fear him and his terrible temper greatly when he is drunk. I fear even more for myself if he should ever discover that what occurred between Edward and I.

I was solemnly walking the cold grounds whilst weeping over the cruel and hateful words that my husband had said. I found Edward sat peacefully beneath a tree near by the wood shed. When he saw me and noticed my distress, he smiled a most beautiful and disarming smile, rose and came to me. He obviously sought to calm me in my distress and pulled me into a warm embrace.

I know not what happened next but one moment my head was buried in the crook of his neck as I sobbed and the next moment, I found that we were kissing most passionately. Not long after, and again I am not sure how it happened, but we were lying together in each other's arms on the cold wet grass, our naked bodies entwined and our garments hastily and clumsily discarded. When we were spent, we lay still, comfortable in each other's loving arms for a while, just looking up at the stars above in the night sky.

Lord Castleleigh continued reading, finding more and more entries of the same type. He read of how they would meet in secret on an almost daily basis. One entry showed and described in disturbing detail of how they had even gone so far as to defile his bed. At some point, it described in some great and sordid detail the meetings between his wife and the wood splitter Edward. He grew more and more angry and disgusted as he learned the details of their affair. He came upon an entry some two months later that left him totally destroyed.

December 28

I am growing most concerned. I have been quite ill in the mornings of late. It has also been over a month and two weeks since my last bleed. What if I am with child? It terrifies me most grievously to what Robert will say or do? I have not been with him intimately since Edward began his work here. I realise what I must do and as much as the thought of it now repulses me, I must and will force myself to lay with him this night; if I am with child, then I will have great news for Robert. He will, if I am lucky, believe that the baby is his.

December 29

I managed to seduce Robert and we were together last night. It was not an act of love and I did not enjoy it. I lay there in disgust and contempt of him.

I could not, would not move, I made no sound or gave no hint of enjoyment or satisfaction and lay quite still while he took me. I was so pleased when he had finished and fell to sleep and the whole while I could not help but wish it was Edward and not my husband grunting repulsively between my thighs.

I know I am wrong but I cannot help it. I think that I am in love with Edward. What am I to do? I would be utterly ruined if any word of our love was to escape. My husband would destroy us both. He cannot know. I feel that I must burn this journal out of fear of its discovery. But I am torn, for it is only here in these pages that I can be honest and confess my deeds and my love.

The journal went on like this. It described Lord Castleleigh's great delight at discovering his wife was finally with child. There were many celebrations and great parties. Lady Castleleigh could not and would not stop her affair with Edward and they would snatch whatever time they could to be together.

All was described by his own wife's foul hand in the journal that he held.

It described the shame she felt at the shape her body took when she began to bloom and how she resented it because it had meant she could not any longer be with Edward until after the birth. She had been quite distraught, she could not confess of the affair to her husband for fear of his reactions and equally, she could not confess to Edward that the baby growing inside of her was his.

The journal went on throughout her pregnancy, how she wished she was not with child and how she wished that she could leave everything behind and run away and be with her Edward for always.

The journal had run out of pages shortly before she had given birth and search as he could, turning their chambers upside down, the lord could find no other of her journals.

From outside, he could hear the unmistakeable sound of the wood splitter working. No thought went through his mind but that of his precious little daughter, Molly. His daughter that so suddenly and so cruelly had been taken from him; he was not her father. She, his beautiful little angel, was not his daughter. The bastard outside splitting logs had seduced his beautiful wife and had given her the child; oh, how he hated his wife at that moment.

He would never forgive her and never tell her that he knew the truth. Molly would never, must never be allowed to know the truth; she would be his daughter again. Lord Castleleigh made up his mind as he wiped unrealised tears from his face that he would remove this Edward from his lands and life forever.

The lord strolled purposely across the lawn towards where the wood splitter stood taking a break. He looked with contempt at the man who had stolen everything from him and decided then and there that his acts would not go unpunished, that he would have revenge on the bastard who had taken all that he held dear in his life away from him.

"Edward," the lord said. "Edward, there is wood in my study that is rotten. It is not good enough and if you wish to keep working here, then you will deal with it at once. I want it removed straightaway."

"Of course, my lord, I will attend to it at once."

He did not even have the courage to meet his lord's eyes as he turned towards the house; this just served to make Lord Castleleigh even angrier. This Edward, not only was he defiling his wife and taking his coin, but he was also a coward. The axe was there, inviting and just lying on the ground by his feet. He did not remember doing it, but all of a sudden, Edward was laid on his stomach, screaming out in both confusion and unimaginable pain with his own axe planted firmly in his back. Lord Castleleigh looked around through tear-blurred eyes; there was no one about to hear the screams and his wife was thankfully out for the day with her aunt. He had to tread down with his foot on Edward's back to get enough leverage to be able to remove the axe. He raised it above his head, showering himself with Edward's blood, and brought it down with every ounce of his strength on the back of Edward's neck with a satisfying thunk.

His aim was true and Edward's head came clean away and rolled over so that Edward stared up at Lord Castleleigh; only in death did he have the courage to meet his eyes, looking up through huge round dead eyes.

The lord spent several busy and stressful hours burying the body behind the stable and clearing up the majority of blood and mess that he had made. He decided that the ants and other wildlife would deal with the rest for him. After the hard work, Lord Castleleigh was sweating and exhausted, but was extremely satisfied with his own deeds.

Molly, his sweet beautiful little Molly, was his once again; he swore to himself that the child would never learn of her mother's affair and would only know him as her one true father. As for his whore of a wife…well, he knew that he would not ever be able to bring himself to lay with her again and if the opportunity should ever arise and present itself…well, he could live with being a widower.

The next day, he would find the most stupid and ugly man imaginable to work for him at splitting wood. He would find someone that the whore would never be attracted to.

Lady Castleleigh would not be allowed to know what had happened to Edward; he would tell her a tale to torture her with. He would tell her that he had run off with some local tavern wench whom he had gotten with bastard child. Let the worthless whore suffer and think that she was not the only foolish woman who had parted her legs for the man, that dear Edward had felt less than nothing towards her; who knew, if he was lucky enough, she may even take her own miserable worthless life.

Lord Castleleigh continued to watch Molly as she laughed and spoke to what he could only assume was some invisible pretend friend. She was getting much too old for such nonsense as this and he would not allow it to continue any further. He stood watching as Molly screwed up her pretty little face and spoke to the nothing again.

"Go on please, please do it again."

"Do what, Molly?"

Startled by the sudden presence of her father, Molly turned around and swiftly climbed to her feet. She looked up into her father's eyes; she almost always felt ashamed and dirty under his gaze.

She was quite worried by what he may say or do to her and her best friend.

"Tell me at once to whom you were talking, child," he commanded her coldly.

Molly reluctantly pointed over to the floor next to where she had been sitting. "Please do not be mad at me, Father. I was but only playing and talking to my friend."

"You are a foolish child, Molly, it is high time that you started to take responsibility; it is time you grew up and started to become a proper lady. There is nobody there, you must stop this nonsense."

Emboldened by her father's obvious silliness, either he had gone blind and could not see her friend or he was playing games with her. Her friend was, to Molly anyway, just as real and solid as she and her father were.

"There he is, Father, just there. We were singing songs together again, just like we used to."

A slight shiver ran up Lord Castleleigh's spine, but he ignored it as he felt his temper starting to rise, along with his voice.

"Who is there? There is no one there. Goddammit, child, what childish game is this that you are trying to play with me? Or do you take me for a great fool, like your mother did?"

Grabbing Molly roughly by her arm, the lord started to drag her forcefully from the room as she began to cry out in distress and pain.

"Daddy, please, please stop it, you're hurting me. Do not do this." She started to beg. "Daddy, do not please, he will not like it. Please, he does not like it when people are being horrible to me."

"Who?" he shouted, his face right close to her own, spittle flying out of his mouth, hitting her in the face. "Who does not like it? Answer me, child, damn you. Tell me." He practically screamed.

Molly just stood still. Her whole little body began to shiver from her head down to her toes. She was just too terrified to move an inch. Something bad, she knew, was going to happen. Lord Castleleigh must have felt it too as he suddenly let go and released Molly.

He stood up straight and looked around the room as a second bigger chill slowly climbed up the length of his spine, turning his skin to gooseflesh. They could both feel the physical change in the temperature as the room plunged colder by several degrees. The lord stood with his mouth agape as Molly slowly turned on the spot and raised her arm to point at the area where she had been sitting.

"The Splitting man, Daddy."

Lord Castleleigh looked to the point where Molly was gesturing at; this time, he really looked. A shadow of uncertainty, maybe even a little fear crossed his intense features. A mist had impossibly risen indoors, slowly turning into dark smoke. The smoke shifted and changed before his eyes; it stretched and became more closely dense as he stood watching. It took on an almost human-like shape. It became a very tall and wide human shape. Still smoke, but a very intimidating human form nonetheless.

"What…What is this madness?" he exclaimed in a very subdued and quiet voice, full of uncertain fear.

"The Splitting man, Daddy. He…he shows me."

"Shows you," he whispered, not a question. "Madness, this is utter madness."

"No, Daddy, it is not. He likes me, you see, he always has. We sing and we play games together and he shows me."

"Shows you what, child? What does he show you?"

"The blood, Daddy, he shows me the blood. There is so much."

"Blood? What…what foolishness is this?"

"Why, he takes his hands off and shows me all the blood."

Lord Castleleigh visibly paled as he sank down to his knees. He looked at Molly but could not believe it. She had been so matter-of-fact about it that there was no room for doubt. She had been telling him the truth the whole time. Her tone said that there was no way she had been making this up. The lord raised his eyes to gaze at the smoke once more, but it had gone, completely disappeared, and the room was now its normal temperature once more.

He knelt down in front of her. "Molly, listen to me. You must not speak ever again to this man; do you understand me? If he comes again, you must tell him to go and to stay gone or I will be most displeased."

Molly looked sadly up at her father. "But he is my only friend, I like him. Please, it is not fair, I have no other friends."

Lord Castleleigh took her gently by the shoulders and brought her into a loving hug, something that he had not done or been able to make himself do since he had found out about his wife's affair with Edward.

"You have me, Molly, and I am all you will ever need. And do not forget that you will be off to school soon. Trust me, my little sweetheart. You do not need this thing for a friend."

He looked into her beautiful wide eyes as the tears began to well up and started to run freely down her cheeks, her lips trembling as she tried to be brave for her daddy.

"Please believe me that it is for your own good. It is only for you that I do this. Now, repeat this after me, Molly. I do not want you, go away."

In her smallest, quietest voice, Molly repeated, "I do not want you, go away."

"Louder, if you please."

"I do not want you, go away."

"Louder."

"I do not want you, go away."

"Louder," he insisted.

"I do not want you, go away," Molly screamed into the room as loud as she could; her tears cascaded down her red face as she commanded her best and only friend in the world to go.

Wondering what was going on with all the noise and what was taking them so long, the maid left the kitchen and went to fetch Lord Castleleigh and his daughter.

"My lord? Miss Molly? Supper is served."

A bloodcurdling scream erupted from the young maid as she walked into the drawing room and saw the bloody devastation before her. She could not have had the time to have taken it all in, as one look and she fainted dead away.

When they were discovered, the lord lay flat on his back on the floor. His face had been sheared off, leaving just a gory red mask of blood and tissue. His hands were gone, literally gone. They were not in the room and even after numerous searches, they were never found. The bloody stumps on the end of his arms where his hands should have been had fountained his blood several feet across the room and up the wall.

He had clearly thrashed about in agony as the spray of his blood was everywhere. Molly's tiny headless body lay next to him. Her small delicate hands were folded peacefully across her chest. There was so much blood that had erupted from the stump that had once been Molly's neck that it still dripped down from the high ceiling. Her head, like her father's hands, was missing and was never found. Blood had covered the room everywhere. The floor was awash with it, the walls had been sprayed scarlet and the ceiling too. It resembled nothing more than a slaughterhouse.

There was so much blood.

Later, the maid had been made to tell of everything that she had both heard and seen before she had fainted. She had told of the man that she had heard laughing long and deep and the sobs of another man, a large man that she had seen crouching down next to the lady Molly with his shoulders shaking as he sobbed. Nobody had believed her mad ravings and she was arrested, tried and found guilty of the murder of Lord Castleleigh and his young daughter, Molly. She had been hung for her crimes, still madly screaming of her innocence and of the evil presence of the others.

Chapter 3
2012 - Sarah

She sat down in her comfortable leather swivel chair at her computer; Sarah shuffled slightly in her seat to get comfortable and started to trawl through her never-ending emails. Running her hand through her thick auburn hair, she began to select and delete the usual rubbish...you know the kind—all the latest offers and money-saving deals. Click, delete, click, delete. When the mouse guided the arrow over the final item in her inbox, Sarah paused. A small smile flickered across her full lips as she sat completely still, staring at the computer screen and read the subject detail:

Haunted and scared, please help us.

Finally, Sarah thought to herself. *Finally, after everything, this is what we have been waiting for.*

Ever since she had been a small child, Sarah had known that she was different from other people. She had experienced feelings and strange paranormal happenings that she would try, but could not explain. Things happened to her that when other people heard would tease her with their disbelief. She had seen things with her own two eyes that other people either could not or did not want to see. Sarah had been the butt of jokes and taunts from other children her age and adults alike.

Sarah's own parents had never really been the paternal type and she had always felt that she was either more of an inconvenience or a prize for them to show off (depending on the time of day, or who was visiting).

As the years progressed and Sarah grew older, she saw and experienced more and more strange happenings but she had also begun to hide these things from others and tried not to tell anyone what she saw and felt as she feared what the reaction would be of the others around her. She realised that people when they found out about her would and in fact did look at her as some kind of freak, a nut job, an attention-seeking teenager with real psychological problems.

When Sarah had turned fourteen, her parents—who had tried to ignore what she said about this taboo subject and had tried to hide first their embarrassment at their odd daughter and then shame that she had brought on them—had decided that enough was enough and that this nonsense must and would stop.

They had made discrete inquiries and had made her seek therapy for her problem; she then had to visit regularly with psychiatrists in the hope that they could 'cure her'. By the time Sarah turned sixteen, she discovered that she found it far easier to lie and confess what they wanted to hear from her instead of telling the truth. She told the doctors that she had made up all of these paranormal experiences that she supposedly had. She confessed that she had made them all up in an effort to gain, selfishly, more attention from her busy parents. It was all lies and deception; she had lied so that she could ruin her hardworking parents' life and gain attention.

By telling them these lies and keeping up this pretence, she had finally managed to rid herself from the psychiatrists. Within a couple of years, the shrinks had declared that they had been successful with her case and thanks to their great and unswerving efforts, she was finally cured. They used that as the justification to charge an enormous fortune in therapy costs to her parents; with their most sincere thanks and gratitude for curing their only daughter, they had managed to secure their position as the defenders and protectors of the delicate minds of impressionable and vulnerable young children.

Satisfied with the apparent outcome, Sarah's parents had treated their daughter and bought Sarah her first computer so that she could lock herself away in her room for hours at a time, and in doing so, keep out of their way. It had actually suited her very well; she was free of the shrinks and could stop telling the lies, get back to who she really was and get on with her normal life, away from the constant disapproving gaze of various adults probing her for her thoughts and feelings on a daily basis.

Sometimes, Sarah would think that it was that first computer of hers that had saved her sanity, but that was just the start of it. Sarah was not by any stretch of the imagination religious but if she did pray, she knew her nightly prayers would always start: Dear lord, we thank you for the internet…

Sarah was no longer alone. Through the internet, social networking, blogs and chatrooms, she found that there were literally millions of people out there in cyber-land just like her.

Because of her past experiences with people's attitude towards her and all the ridicule she had had to endure, Sarah had never had the courage to use her real name on any of the sites. She was just so delighted that there were so many people out there that had also seen and experienced both the strange and the paranormal just as she had. She would chat to other users for hours, sharing experiences, seeking advice on how to deal with what she saw and even on some rare occasions, offering advice to others.

Sarah had at last found her place in the world.

Through the internet, she found hundreds of online meetings for psychics, medium chatrooms, haunted locations, ghost hunts, ghost walks and so on and so forth. Sarah just loved to search through all these sites and read and learn everything that she possibly could on the paranormal; it had become her love and her one true passion in life.

By the time she was twenty, Sarah had managed to move out of her parents' home, leaving all the bad memories, into her own flat. She managed it mainly thanks to her parents' generosity, or, as she suspected, more to do with her parents wanting their own space back and being prepared to pay for it. It was through one of her chatrooms that she had first discovered the 'Ghosts are with us' paranormal group.

It was a real group, not just an online chat. The group was moving from town to town across the country, picking up massive popularity as it went. Sarah did many searches on the travelling group and found numerous newspaper articles and even local news reports on the group as they travelled through the towns and cities. 'Ghosts are with us' even had their own website and advertised the upcoming dates and locations that they would be visiting. Sarah had almost fallen from her chair when she saw that they would be visiting a town only twelve miles away in less than a week's time. Sarah knew she must go to it.

A shy young Sarah had caught the train into town and walked down street after street until she came across the town hall where the event was taking place. Taking a deep breath, closing her eyes and steeling herself, Sarah walked slowly into the town hall as she pushed through the doors with posters advertising:

Ghosts Are with Us
Tonight at 8:00 pm
Come and join us for an evening of spiritual discussion and enlightenment of the soul.
Share your experiences with us and listen to the tales of others.
Come and find a loved one; find peace and understanding
£5.00 entry
We can't wait to see you

Sarah walked into the main hall and stopped; she stared around in wonder at all the people who were already there. There must have been over fifty people mingling and talking, sharing their own personal experiences. She saw an elderly silver-haired lady sat on a plastic chair behind a table with a book of tickets and an ice cream tub with cash in it.

Sarah paid the lady her five-pound entry fee and started to explore. The evening lasted for just over two hours; in that time, she listened whilst people spoke to the audience and told of their experiences; she had met several very interesting characters who she was most fascinated with.

What a wonderful change that had made, spending time with so many people like herself, others who were not afraid to say what they thought and did not have to hide their feelings. That was also the evening that she met Tom.

Tom was the same age as Sarah. Give or take a few months. He was tall and handsome with a mop of dark hair upon his head. He would listen to Sarah as she spoke; they shared many things in common but he also shared her passions and most important of all, he understood her and she found that she could actually talk openly and honestly to him.

Over the course of several months, Sarah found herself travelling up and down the country, attending more and more of these events. She loved the company of these people and was just like a sponge, she soaked up as much information and advice about the paranormal as she could. Of course, the added bonus for her was that she was able to see and spend more time with Tom as well.

Soon, they would meet outside of the meetings, they would hook up for weekends together and before long, Tom had moved in and they lived together in Sarah's flat. Sarah put it to Tom one day that they had gotten so much from each other and that she had learnt so much that she wanted to use all that she had learned and start helping others as well. She knew how hard it was to break away from the taunts and the persecution of being a believer.

Tom had eagerly jumped at the chance; together and with new-found friends, they organised their own paranormal investigation group and decided to give their help to whoever asked for their help and that they would never ever allow others to feel as alone and disbelieved as they once had. Sarah and Tom's group consisted of just five members.

Together, they would go and investigate any claims of hauntings or paranormal activity that they received. They would gather as much evidence as they could and present it to their clients. From there, they would advise as best they could on what was happening at the location and how best for the client to deal with the situation from that point onwards.

Apart from Sarah and Tom, who were the head investigators and the two who decided what cases they should take on and sort out the crank and hoaxes from the real thing, Tom invited his old friend Andrew to join them. Andrew was a real gadget geek; it was him who helped them purchase their video and night vision cameras and the audio recording devices, not to mention all the software to help them analyse their findings.

Sarah had not been too sure about Andrew at first as he was a complete non-believer and welcomed it as a great chance for him to disprove the presence of ghosts. Tom had talked her into using him though, and together they realised that it was a good idea to have a real sceptic like Andrew around to help them stay grounded and ensure that they would properly prove or disprove things. Also, they thought that if they could convert him and make a believer out of him, they knew that they would be successful.

Along with Andrew came Jessica, Andrew's younger sister, who was so keen to seek out any paranormal goings on. As a self-confessed fan of television shows about paranormal investigations, she was so eager to learn and go to haunted places for first-hand experiences that she could not do enough to help out.

Jessica reminded Sarah of herself when she started attending meetings and the girl would listen and learn whenever she could; she was so far a very valuable addition to their group.

Jessica would tell them all about the various television shows that she watched (she admitted that some were obviously fakes and con artists, but others were definitely the real deal) and insisted that if they wanted people to take them seriously, they would have to find a spiritualist medium to join them in their investigations, someone who could actually talk to the spirits and would help convince their clients.

Sarah was not convinced that this was a good idea but she allowed herself to go along with it as she, Tom and Andrew developed an online advertisement for their group, asking for a psychic medium to join them. It took several weeks, but eventually their advertisement received a response.

Paul Ackermann replied to the advertisement they had posted on the internet and came to join them. Andrew did not take well to Paul as he would supposedly start talking to 'spirits' whilst they were meeting; he was not shy of vocalising that he was not at all convinced of Paul's integrity or honesty in his claims to be able to communicate with those that had passed.

Sarah herself was not convinced either, she knew herself that there were a lot of con artists out there who would prey on the weak and hopeful, delivering false hope and comfort to them whilst simultaneously robbing them blind. She decided however to give Paul a chance, but to keep a close eye on him. All the years that she had been made to endure cruel taunts of others had made her wary but she decided that she must be prepared to give others a chance. That much she had learned.

Thanks to Andrew and his skills on the computer and internet, he had devised and designed, built and published a fantastic website for them. The website introduced all five members of the group and gave a brief history of them all. In the site, it explained that they were not alone and they had no need to fear the disbelievers and their harsh scorns and ridicule. They now had somewhere to turn to for help. Sarah, Tom, Andrew, Jessica and Paul were there for them to give help and advice to all those who asked for it.

Haunted Hunters was born.

Sarah clicked open and read her email: Haunted and scared, please help.

```
Dear Haunted Hunters,
    Let me start by saying that my family and I are
terrified. We do not know who, or where to turn. We
have had some very strange and scary things happen in
our new home. I really hope that you can help us.

Susan Phillips (Mrs)
```

Sarah read and re-read the email cry for help several times before she called Tom in to have a look at it.

"Tom, have you got a moment, Hun? We got an email."

Tom put down the latest Terence Byford novel, *Stray into Darkness*, that he was reading and wandered slowly into the room, glass of whisky in hand. He looked at Sarah from his deep green eyes, admiring the lady in his life. "Welcome to the 21st century, sweetheart, we get emails all the time," he joked.

Refusing to rise to or, as she would say, 'lower herself' to his level, Sarah frowned at Tom and pointed at the computer monitor. "Not us, I mean Haunted Hunters has received an email. Can you believe it, it's our first one."

"Hmmm," Tom said as he moved in close to read the message. "What do you think, babe? Think it's genuine? I mean, Andrew only just got this site up and running yesterday."

"I...I don't know. What do you think? Shall I reply?"

"Well, best had, love, otherwise there is no point in advertising, is there?"

Tom put his hand on her shoulder as Sarah turned back to her computer and typed:

```
Dear Mrs Phillips,
    Thank you for your email. I am so sorry to hear of
the fear that you and your family are feeling. First
let me tell you that you are not alone, we are here to
listen to you and help you in any way we can.
    From your message, I understand that you have a new
house. Could you please give us some bullet points on
what seems to be happening in your property and also
any history that you may know of, the area in general?
    I look forward to your response.

Sarah Jackson
(Co-Founder, Haunted Hunters)
```

Sarah turned her head to look up at Tom. He nodded, so she clicked send.

"I doubt whether we will get an answer tonight," Sarah said. "I'm going to go and put the kettle on. Do you want a cup of coffee?"

"No thanks, Hun, I will nurse this a bit longer." He smiled as he swirled the amber liquid around in his glass and took an appreciative sip.

Sarah decided to busy herself in the kitchen. She put the kettle on and put a spoonful of coffee granules in her mug. Checking the time, Sarah noticed that it was very nearly eight o'clock. She decided to sit down with her cup of coffee and watch her favourite detective programme for an hour and then check her emails again, mainly in the hope of hearing something more from Mrs Phillips. She really hoped that it was something genuine and not someone out to make fun of them and waste their time.

At about quarter to nine, when the last advert break came on, Sarah could not resist any longer so she walked through to her office space and woke the computer. She opened her email inbox and found one new email waiting for her. Its subject: `Please help us.`

Sarah wasted no time; she ran to get Tom and together, they sat down in front of the computer monitor and read:

```
Dear Miss Jackson,
    Thank you so much for responding to my call for
help. My husband Brandon has told me to say that you
must take us seriously. You are our last hope and we
do not know who else to turn to. I will not waste your
time with meaningless waffle so I will bullet our
problems as you asked.
    *I myself have gone to have a bath; I would turn the
taps on and go to undress. On several occasions, I have
returned to find my bath filled with blood. Each time
I have run to tell my husband but when he comes to see,
it is always full of steaming water.
    *When sat at my dressing table removing make-up or
brushing my hair out, I have seen a horribly twisted
and disfigured man standing behind me in the mirror.
So far, whenever I turn around, he is gone.
    *My last and most terrifying has only happened once
and this was last night. Brandon filled the bath for
me as I was too scared it would be blood. He left me
when I got in for a soak. Brandon had come quickly,
running back up when from downstairs, he could hear me
thrashing about in the water and banging as I kicked
the bathtub. I had laid back to relax when all of a
```

sudden, I felt two large strong hands hold me by my throat and force me down under the water. Absolutely terrified for my life, I struggled and grabbed at the wrists but it was only when Brandon pulled me out did the pressure disappear from my throat.

*My husband Brandon came home from work last week and when he walked into the sitting room, he was witness to a woman bent over and repeatedly stabbing a man again and again whilst he lay there. Brandon ran out of the house and called the police. When the police arrived, Brandon took them inside and they then threatened to arrest him for wasting police time. There was no evidence of anyone ever being in there.

*This next has happened twice. Our fourteen-year-old daughter, Alice, has woken up in the night to find herself stripped of her nightgown, naked and tied up with rope. She would be gagged with an old rag and can see a very well-dressed man standing over her with a whip in his hand.

*Lastly, my daughter Alice again. The previous has happened twice as I said. It has not happened for a week now, but every morning when she awakes, Alice says that she can see a huge man standing by her bed with his back to her. When she sits up, he will turn around, smile at her, hold out and show her the bloody stumps where his hands are missing. She runs into our room screaming.

As to the history of the area, I know of nothing. There have been stories of vicious killings in the village and a nearby town a hundred years or more ago, some also as recently as fifty years ago. I have not listened too much and dismissed them as idle gossip. Now, I am not so sure.

We moved into the house nearly two months ago and it is only this last month that things have really started to happen.

We need help, we cannot explain what is happening or why but because of what is happening, we cannot remain here much longer. The house has now been put back on the market but who knows when it will sell in the financial climate today. PLEASE HELP US.

Susan

Sarah looked at Tom, he was white, and judging by the look that he gave her suggested that she was as well. Finally, she managed to find her voice.

"Tom, we have to help these poor people. My god, what they are going through. I never imagined we would get caught up in things like this."

She hugged Tom as he stroked her hair and back.

"Me neither, my god, this is awful. Email her back, love, get her address and I will contact the guys. Tell her we will be over Friday evening. Tell her we will do absolutely everything that we possibly can for them. Tell her we will need the house to ourselves for the night and that they should book themselves into a hotel for that night."

Sarah nodded as she turned uncertainly back to the keyboard.

My dear Susan,

What you have told me is truly disturbing. Let me assure you that we will do everything in our power to help you. It is Tuesday today; if you are agreeable, my team and I will come this Friday evening; that will give us time to research your area and get organised. I strongly recommend that you and your family stay in either a hotel or with friends that night as we will need the complete run of your house. Here is what we intend to do:

- We will set up equipment around your house and try to communicate with whatever or whoever is there.
- Paul (our medium) will try to find out what it is that they want.

- We will record with audio and video so we can check and back up anything that we may find.
- We will then need to analyse our findings.
- We will come back to you as soon as we can and show you our findings; we will do our best to advise you on how best to proceed and what you will need to do from that point onwards.

I hope this is all agreeable to you. Please email me your address and any other information that you think we may need.

Do not worry, we <u>will</u> help you.

Sarah

It was no more than five minutes later when Sarah got her reply. Susan had agreed to everything that Sarah had asked of her and would be there to welcome them and show them around on Friday. In the meantime, she would book her family into the local hotel. She could come up with nothing of any further help in explaining the history of what was happening in their house. She had included her address and also an attachment that Sarah clicked on and opened. There was a heading: Brandon took this photo of my neck after he got me out of the bath.

Sarah looked carefully at the photograph. She could see a pale neck cold with goose bumps and wet with the soapy water, but she could also see the dark tell-tale bruises. Finger marks around the throat where the attacker had tried to strangle and hold Susan Phillips under the water.

A chill climbed Sarah's back, raising her own goose bumps as she listened to Tom calling the others; he was telling them about the case. He asked Andrew to look into the history of the area and asked that Jessica help him. When he telephoned Paul, the medium was horrified at what he was told about the Phillips family and what they had to endure. He pledged to help them as much as he could to get to the bottom of what was happening. Sarah sat still in silence as she questioned herself on what exactly they were getting themselves into.

Chapter 4
1834 – William

They appeared to make the most handsome of couples, him with his expensive suit and large tailored overcoat and her in her best evening gown and cloak. It was a very cold and damp dark evening as the couple made their way quietly down the streets and roads and through a dark wooded track towards the large house at the edge of the town. The words they spoke to each other were visible mist as they breathed out into the cold night air.

"Oh, William, you really are just such an absolute gentleman. It is so very kind of you to walk me home, what with my husband being away on his business. I do so find it very unnerving walking out here alone at this late an hour."

"Believe me, Mrs Farrow, it is no effort at all, and it is my honest pleasure to make sure a beautiful lady such as you gets to her home in safety."

She turned to face William as they reached the doorstep. He was such a handsome, well-dressed and kindly gentleman, so polite and helpful to her when her husband was away that she could not resist inviting him inside.

"Please, William, I insist; as I have said before, you must please call me Emily. Now we have arrived all safe and sound, can I presume to ask if you would care for a small tipple before you must go?"

A dark look flickered across his features; it was there but for a second, no more. He glanced over to Emily with his warmest and most sincere smile. "Very well, Mrs…Emily; that is most generous of you and would be most appreciated. I would be totally delighted to accept your most generous offer."

Mrs Farrow turned from him then; she was thankful for the dark as she was flushed and blushing furiously at the thought of entertaining such a gentleman in her home. She opened the heavy oak front door and taking William by the arm, led him inside. Once inside the parlour, she led him over to the large overstuffed armchair by the fireplace and gestured for William to sit.

"Please, William, have a seat. I will not be long in fetching you your drink."

William sat comfortably on the chair, watching, studying Emily with a keen appreciation as she busied herself preparing his drink. He so liked to watch women, especially beautiful women like Emily. To look at her was most peaceful; he just loved the way her long dark curls hung down to below her shoulders. She had a wonderful slim figure; she was curvaceous and most delicately enchanting. Her long flowing dress covered her for the most part, something that William found most alluring in his women.

Smiling the sweetest of smiles, Emily handed William a stunningly engraved crystal glass, half full with a deep amber-coloured liquid. Just as she put the glass into William's hand, he let it fall clumsily from his fingers to smash on the hardwood floor.

Making a big show of being apologetic, he said, "My dear Emily, I am so terribly sorry, please I beg you, forgive me my silly clumsiness. I am such a fool; please do allow me to clean this mess up."

Emily would hear none of it and certainly would not allow her guest, not her sweet William, to be put out. Just as she bent down to pick up the pieces of broken glass, she said happily, "No, really, William; it is fine, after all, these little accidents do happen. I will just—"

Emily Farrow never got the chance to finish what she was saying as William shot to his feet beside her whilst pulling a dark truncheon out from his overcoat pocket and bludgeoning her hard across the back of her pretty neck.

He looked down on Emily. "Now then, my most lovely and most dear sweet Emily," William said to the inert body lying at his feet, rubbing his hands together as the dark look came to his face once more, this time to stay. "Now we will have us a most pleasurable night to remember. Or at least, I will. I am however most certain though that you, my dear, will probably not live long enough to ever see another sunrise."

William crouched down beside Emily's prone body, a wild look in his wide staring eyes. He began to sweat and his hands shook in anticipation as he began slowly and methodically to unlace her bodice and remove the clothes from her unconscious person.

Emily had the strangest sensation; she was not sure whether she was asleep or awake. Try as she might, she could not open her eyes, therefore she decided that she must indeed still be asleep and dreaming. The dream was a very strange one for her, she was cold and shivering. It felt as though she was lying on a very cold and very hard bed that made her whole body ache. Her arms were pulled tightly together above her head and it felt like her feet had been bound. Emily could hear footsteps moving around her. *Am I still sleeping?* she asked herself again.

"Emily."

From some distant place, she could hear someone calling out to her. Was it her husband? No, it could not be as he was away on business. William then. *Oh goodness*, she thought. *William, what did we do last night?* Worry started to creep into her still fuzzy mind, the last thing that she remembered was giving William his glass of drink. She heard it again.

"Emily."

That voice sounded so close and familiar; she knew it.

"Arrrrgggghhhh."

Emily screamed out in agony as a white-hot pain raked itself across her chest. Her eyes flew open with the pain. She had not been asleep. She had not been dreaming. As the pain began to subside, leaving a hot throbbing sensation where it had been, Emily tried to lift her head slowly and take in her surroundings through tear-blurred vision.

It took but a second for her to realise that the cold hard surface on which she lay was in fact the floor of the cellar under her house. Panic began to creep in as it ran over her and entered her body. Her bare arms were stretched beyond her head, bound tightly with rope. Emily looked down the length of her body; horrified, she realised that she was as naked as the day she was born and with no way to cover her nakedness.

She was both furious that this had been so cruelly done to her but also ashamed as well. No one but her husband should see her like this. It is amazing the irrational thoughts that enter our heads in times of great distress, as Emily was discovering for herself as she continued to look down the length of her body. She saw an angry red welt across her breast where something long and thin had struck her; she saw what looked like teeth marks around her nipples as well. *But who would?* Further down her body, she could see that her legs were bound together at the ankles, also with rope.

"Emily."

Her head snapped to the left. *Oh dear lord, no, not you*, she thought to herself as she lost control of her bladder, feeling ashamed once more as the floor began to warm beneath her. William was stood just off to the side of her, smiling his handsome smile down at her with a whip in his hand.

It suddenly struck her then; it was William, sweet William, the kindly gentleman that had done this so cruel and humiliating thing to her. It was William that had gained her trust and abused her. It was William that had stripped her of all her dignity. It was William that hurt her and whipped her chest.

Emily began to sob as the realisation of what was happening and what might happen to her sank in. The danger was real; William could and most probably would kill her. At that thought, the real shakes took hold of her; Emily shook as if she had just been placed in a freezer.

"So, you're finally with us again, are you?" William spoke with a cold dark voice, a voice that held absolutely no emotion at all.

Emily for her part could not hope to respond. All she could do was sob and shiver in her state of absolute and complete terror.

William crouched down, putting his hands either side of her head and leaning in close so that his handsome but twistedly evil face was breathing a foul stench at her, mere inches from her tear-streaked face.

"What is wrong, my love? You do not want to talk to me today? A shame to be sure; a few hours ago, you were all but throwing yourself at me. But now…still, it does not matter; there is more than one way to communicate with you. If you will not talk to me freely, then that is fine. But you will scream to me. That, I can promise you."

Reaching into his pocket, William retrieved an old dirty handkerchief whilst simultaneously dropping the whip. She watched it fall near her side and tried to move her head away from him as she realised what he intended to do with his handkerchief. He grasped Emily's shaking, denying head to hold it still, struggling with her thrashing as he twisted around to hold it steady and tight between his knees, applying as much pressure against her skull as he could and pinched her nose hard and twisted it until it began to bleed and she opened her mouth to scream. Instead of a scream though, only a weak muffled sound came out as he shoved and stuffed the old handkerchief into her now open mouth.

William stood up and walked away from her. Emily could hear his grunts and curses as he began to work with some ropes or other such things. She was not sure what he was doing; she was only glad that for the moment he was not hurting her.

Her arms involuntarily raised above her head as her body began to drag along the rough floor. She could feel the skin of her back and rump furrowing as she was dragged. It did not last long; just as fresh tears began to fall, her body rose up into the air to join her arms. Before Emily knew it, she was stood upright.

William tied the rope off to ensure she could not move or fall. He was talking and muttering things to himself as he walked slowly around her in inspection. He was leering at her and painfully poking at her every now and then.

William stopped behind her; she could feel his warm breath on her ear as her skin turned to gooseflesh. He placed his hands softly on her shoulders and ran them lightly, almost tenderly as a lover would, down her sides to her hips, causing her fear to escalate with mixed feelings of and for this man, accompanied with more shaking and shivering.

She was his. She had been his since he asked to walk her home. He could do whatever he pleased with her and she was utterly powerless to prevent him doing it. Tears and mucus mingled with the blood from her nose as he slid around her body to look into her eyes. He loved to look in their eyes; he loved to see the terror and helplessness floating in them. "Are you scared, Emily?" She did not respond.

"Do you know what I'm going to do to you, Emily?"

She managed a shake of her head.

"Do you think I am going to rape you, Emily?"

If it were possible, her eyes widened even further at the terror at his words. He spat in her face.

"Do not flatter yourself. I may be what you might call sick, and I may be what you might consider evil but if you think that I would defile myself with the likes of you, then you are most surely mistaken. It is true that I love women. I love women most deeply. I love the body you women own; it is exciting. It is true that I make love to women. But I do it in my own way, not some disgusting act of the joining of bodies that you would have me do.

"Oh no. Let me tell you what arouses me, Emily. Your blood, your pain and your suffering. Oh yes, and your slow death as well is my climax. Oh, you will be my lover, Emily. I will make you bleed. I will hurt you most severely and you will suffer dearly for it. You will be in more pain than you ever thought would be possible and I will keep you conscious so that you may suffer through it all. And when I climax with the end of our lovemaking, I will endow upon you death's most sweetest kiss. You will beg for it and you will promise me anything I want, but that is rude, a man must climax only when he is ready."

For the second time, Emily lost control and could feel the warm liquid as it trickled down her legs to pool on the floor around her feet. He looked at the mess she was making on the floor and he mocked her cruelly for her weak womanly ways, as he laughed hard and deep in her face.

William took a step backwards and bent to pick up his previously discarded whip. He looked lovingly at the carved ivory handle, caressing the bulbous end. He stroked the length of the handle, feeling the vein-like ridges beneath his fingers. Holding the handle tightly in his grip, he let the three, twenty-inch lengths of leather uncoil to the floor. Each end had three tight knots in it so as to inflict more pain and damage.

Swinging his arm back, he let fly with the whip at her as if he was some great showman or lion tamer. He struck her once, twice, three times. He struck her arms, her breasts again and her legs. He danced all around her whilst lashing out with his long leather tongue time and time again. He got her face; he whipped her neck and rump.

William used the whip and tore into her back and sides and stomach. He whipped her brutally all over. William stopped his lovemaking to regain his breath and also that he may admire his handiwork. He stared appreciatively at her, welts and tears that were crisscrossing all over her once stunning body. Blood flowed from her and mixed with her own urine at her feet.

Emily managed to spit the filthy and bloody handkerchief out and scream. Fresh blood flowed freely from her mouth where she had bitten her tongue and lips against the great pains that she had so far endured. She screamed as William whipped. She screamed as the blood flowed from her torn body. She screamed until her voice had left her throat raw and bloody from her efforts and she could scream no more. Still William danced, around and around her in his sadistic lovemaking dance.

Emily could no longer feel the fresh pain being inflicted on her; she was just one huge ball of agony from the beatings she had taken so far. How she stayed conscious she did not know. Emily only managed to stay on her feet because of the rope that held her upright; elsewise, she would have collapsed into oblivion long ago.

"Did you enjoy that, my love?"

William was there in front of her. *Thank god*, she thought, *he has stopped whipping me, stopped hurting me. When did he stop?*

"W…Wil…Will…Pu…Puhl…"

"Shut up." William backhanded her hard across the face but Emily did not even feel it amongst all the other hurts.

"Good, you can still beg. Oh, I do like that. Do you like the pain, oh my love, but is it not divine? Look how aroused you have made me."

Emily could not see anything until William stepped away from her. Only then did she realise that at some point, he had removed his clothes. *My god, he is going to use that thing on me.* She saw him holding his erection; huge and solid and pointing it at her. *He loves this, he loves my agony. Please stop it, kill me and end it now. I want no more. Why, William, why?*

"Emily."

She came back to herself and looked up to see his face so close to her. Emily tried to recoil away from the William monster in fear but she just could not move. She was helpless before him. Emily looked and she could see his deep cold eyes, so deep and cold they were that they appeared to have no bottom to their evil depths.

Something caught the light as it moved in front of her face. *It…it's shiny. How pretty it is. I like it when it shines.* "Can I have it, William?" Emily was delirious; unsure of what it was she was seeing, or saying.

"My knife? You want my knife, Emily? Well yes, my love, you shall have it, but first, we will love each other with it."

Knife, what knife? No. Emily did not understand what she was saying or what was being said to her. *Someone has their hand on my breast.* William bent down and almost lovingly cradled and caressed her bloody breasts. He cupped one in his hand almost lovingly and lifted it gently as he began to cut.

Emily could feel nothing of what William was doing to her now except for a light pressure upon her breast. *He is so gentle, so loving. Hmmm, William, that's so nice.*

William's tongue was stuck out from the side of his mouth in concentration as sweat started to bead on his forehead. The first cut was very shallow as he expertly but gently and carefully guided his long carving knife all the way around Emily's nipple. Blood formed around the cut and slowly rolled down her breast and onto his hand still firmly holding it. *Oh my, William, that hurts but hmmm, it's good, it feels so good.*

"This may hurt somewhat, my sweet," he whispered into her ear, smiling. "But love does hurt, does it not?"

Hmmm, hmmm, William yes, that's…Ow, no, stop, no…"NO." Emily threw her head back in a scream to wake the dead, or at least it would have been a scream if her vocal cords were not already wasted by all of her previous screams. Instead, it came out as more of a weakened and pained croak.

William had to hold on to her tightly as she struggled and thrashed in pain against him. William was impressed however by the resilience of the woman; her strength was amazing, and that she was still able to struggle at this stage of their lovemaking was nothing short of a miracle. Still, William could not stand for her to be struggling.

He rose to his feet, letting go of her and smashed Emily as hard as he could in the face. He felt the bones break as her nose gave way beneath his fist and groaned in excitement as he saw fresh blood begin to flow from her ruined nose.

"This behaviour of yours just will not do, my love," William said to Emily's slumped and now quiet, unmoving body. He knew that she was conscious as he could see her eyes open, looking with a deep loathing that he took for love. "If you keep up this foolish struggling of yours, then my loving cuts will not be precise as they should be and I will be forced to hurt you. Please my lady, do not oppose my love, embrace it and receive the pleasure I am trying to give you."

William stuck his face right up into Emily's once more so that their foreheads were touching and he growled darkly at her. "I will warn you this one time, if you struggle again, I will remove your pretty lips. Struggle again; it will be your ears. If you struggle against me a third time, then I will rip and tear your pretty eyelids from your face."

Leaning in and grabbing roughly at her bloody and sweaty slippery breast, William began to carve his love into Emily once more. He sliced from her nipple, straight up until the knife tip reached her breast bone. Biting down and through her lip, Emily tasted fresh blood in her mouth as she struggled as hard as she could against moving, for fear of what he would do to her.

William brought his knife back to the bottom of Emily's nipple and sliced down following the delicious curve of her full breast. The quiet sounds of whimpering and sobbing that Emily was making was most pleasing to William and he allowed himself a pleasurable smile as he licked the dripping blood from her breast.

Please William, I cannot take this anymore. Please, for the love of our lord, I beg you. Please William…ple—

Placing the point of the carving knife to the side of her nipple, he sliced around to the top of her ribcage under her arm. He came back to the nipple for the last time to cut across and down to the centre of her cleavage between the breasts; there, he stopped and stood back to admire his work.

"Yes, oh my, yes. Look at you, my sweet." He dropped the knife to the floor and clasped his hands together and grinned in excitement as a child would wait for a Christmas gift. He moved close to her, his erect penis poking her gently in the belly as he reached for her bloody breast.

Carefully, he pinched her nipple between his forefinger and thumb as he rubbed and eased the skin back that he had cut away from her breast. Slowly, it came as William peeled Emily's breast like a ripe banana. He peeled the quarters that he had sliced until her breast was left bare of its skin. Bending down to retrieve his knife once more William licked his lips, still bloody from his tasting of Emily earlier.

Carefully, oh so carefully, he held the loose flaps of skin away from her body whilst slicing them away as close to her body as he could. William stood back once again to admire his beautiful Emily. He loved the way her breasts looked, one smooth and firm and pink whilst the other contrasted with it perfectly, a beautiful mound of red fat and tissue with a nipple standing hard and proud in the centre. It dripped blood down onto Emily's stomach and rolled down her body, as it hung next to its bland and pale twin.

"Oh my love," William exclaimed. "Look at you, my sweet; you are so very beautiful, look what I have done for you. Hmm, I can feel it building, can you? Aahh, the climax is coming, my love; yes, it is close now, so very close."

When Emily did not respond to William's loving and soothing voice, he knew that something was wrong. He ran to her and grabbed hold of her roughly by the shoulders and shook her so hard that her unconscious head flew from side to side.

At some point, the pain and suffering had become too much for Emily to endure. She had given in to the sweet escape of unconsciousness. *How can she do this to me? What is wrong with the damn unappreciative woman?* he thought. To fall asleep during his lovemaking was just unforgivable. His hands became fists as he raised them tightly to the side of his head as he shook it from side to side in a silent denial; this was all wrong.

"No, no, no, no, no. This will not do, Emily. This will not do at all," he told her in a voice so low and full of dread that it was a good thing she was still unconscious and unable to hear him.

William broke then, he broke into one of his mad dances as he scooped up the carving knife and whip from the floor beside him and went at Emily. He would cut her and slice at her, remove slices of skin from her. He would whip her raw and whip her where she was already raw. He even pissed on her and into her severe wounds; still, she just hung there. After nearly ten minutes of this, William was exhausted and the sweat was literally pouring off him.

He must stop, he realised, he could not climax until Emily was awake, he must regain control of himself and calm down. William sat down cross-legged at Emily's feet, he either did not care or did not realise what it was that he was sitting in. He sat still with his head hung as his breathing slowed and he relaxed next to the once beautiful Emily Farrow, who now looked nothing more than a piece of meat that you would expect to see hanging in the butcher's window. William was not the most patient of men, but wait he would. He needed desperately to climax their lovemaking but would not allow it yet; no, she must be awake.

What? Where...where am I? Emily was slowly coming back to consciousness. To start with, there was no pain. Her body had done its best protecting her from that agony as she had slept. Slowly though, very slowly, the excruciating pain was returning once more to her shattered and broken body. Her arms felt like they were coming out of their sockets where they met her burning shoulders. Her face felt like it was on fire as did her neck and back and sides.

My legs. Where are my legs? He took, he has taken my legs. She had no feeling at all in her legs, no feeling below her waist. She had no idea what he had done to her but being unable to move or to open her eyes, she could not see whether or not she still had them.

Her right breast felt as if someone had poured acid on it, yet strangely there was still a cool draft blowing gently on her nipple that she could feel was hard and puckered. If she could have made any noise, she probably would have laughed at her nipple as it betrayed the rest of her body by being turned on by what was happening to her.

Slowly and gritting her teeth through the agony, Emily managed to open her eyes. Her head dropped forward to face down her body. Still, she could not see her legs; all she could see was her upper body, a mass of red, ripped and torn flesh and her beautiful breast. What had the monster done to her? *Why William? I wanted you. I wanted to love you, my gentle, sweet and handsome William.*

A lone tear rolled from her bloodshot eye down to the smashed ruin that had once been her nose.

It hung there for a second or two before falling. It fell down and down, past her ruined body and landed in a slight splash upon William's shoulder. He stirred immediately upon feeling it. He looked up and their eyes met. William's head slowly leaned to one side as he smiled a cruel thin-lipped smile up at his love.

"My sweet, you're back, are you ready?" he asked as he climbed to his feet. "Shall we climax together?" he asked as his lips brushed lightly against her own split, chewed and ruined lips.

She did not feel the pressure or pain as the large carving knife pushed at and then entered her body at her navel. She did not feel her body lift and jerk as he, with incredible strength, ripped her open from her navel to her throat. She did not feel as her organs and intestines spilt, unravelled and fell from her body to gather in a red heap on the floor at her feet. She did not feel or hear as William let out one last huge gasp of absolute pleasure as he ejaculated his evil seed directly into her torn-open body.

"Did you enjoy that, my love?" William gasped at Emily. He was breathless, he was spent. He sat down in all of her bodily fluids and innards to rest. "I love you, Emily Farrow," he declared as sleep descended and took him.

Emily thought or felt no more as her all too short life left her.

"What is this? Untie me now. Who are you? What…Help me, somebody help me. Who tied me up? Where are you? Talk to me, goddamn you. What do you want with me? Who are you? Where are you?"

William slipped and slithered around in all the blood that he had spilt. He was bound tightly at hand and foot. He could move and wriggle but he could not find his feet. A blind panic gripped him tightly as he shouted for his tormentor. How long he laid shouting he did not know. He was hoarse from shouting and his naked body raw with his writhing around on the rough cellar floor.

But it was only when he saw the big carving knife coming for him, his carving knife, in the hand of Emily Farrow, that he lost it. The knife shined brightly as it caught the light. She brought it in front of his eyes so that he was left in no doubt of what was going to happen. That was when he lost control completely and pissed and shit himself.

"You, sir, are a sick bastard. That butchered thing that you left hanging there is…was my twin sister. So tell me, how does it feel to be at the mercy of someone else? To be helpless and scared, you twisted little freak? Now you know what she felt. How does it feel to know you are going to die?"

William looked up; his mouth hung open as he stared into Emily's eyes. *How? We loved and you died. How my love? How?*

William had not realised that Emily had her sister staying in the house with her whilst her husband was away. But William did manage to find his voice once more as Emily's twin bent over him and grabbed roughly, turning him onto his back. "Lie still," she hissed at him through her teeth as she took hold of his flaccid penis and sliced clean through it at a point two thirds down its length.

He screamed at her, he begged and pleaded with her and promised her anything as his stump pissed blood all over himself. All of his agonised pleas fell on deaf ears and turned into muffled agonised cries as Julia savagely shoved and forced his dead member into his mouth, breaking a few of his teeth along the way with the force of her pushing, as far as she could.

William began to gag and choke on himself as she raised the carving knife high once more, bringing it down and stabbed him repeatedly over and over. He tried to scream until his last ragged breath. *I love you.* And he did.

Covered in William's blood, Emily's twin sister stood over him, glaring down in disgust at the monster that had savaged Emily.

Julia crossed the room and she went to her sister. She cut her down and laid her peacefully on the floor, crossing her torn arms carefully upon her ruined chest. She gave her sister a last kiss on her bloody brow and slowly turned, with deep hatred and sorrow in her eyes she walked back to William's mutilated dead body.

Tears flowed fast and freely down her cheeks as she spoke, "You may have killed her in this life, but I killed you. I own your spirit now. I will follow you into the next life and all others and will always be there to guard my sweet sister from you. I will pursue you for the rest of time if I must, killing you over and over again."

Julia Farrow plunged the carving knife deep into her own heart and collapsed down upon William, claiming him as hers from that moment onwards.

Chapter 5
2012 – Sarah

The Ford Galaxy was speeding along the M5 motorway on the long journey down to the south coast and Dorset, to the family home of the Phillips, in the county town of Dorchester.

Sarah sat upfront in the passenger seat next to Tom who was driving. Andrew and Jessica were sat in the back (or what was the middle really), with all of their video and sound equipment for the investigation on the backseat and their personal stuff in the luggage area. Sarah was still concerned that they may be wasting their time and heading all this way for nothing. The team though had stood behind her decision to come and had agreed to back her and do all they could to help these people.

There was something about Mrs Phillips though; some strange thing that gave Sarah chills every time she thought about the family and the destination that they were rapidly approaching. She was excited that they were finally going to do what they had planned for so long—a proper investigation—and try to help a family in paranormal distress.

It was most unnerving though as the claims that Mrs Phillips had put forward were a lot more extreme and terrifying than any that Sarah herself had ever experienced, and these were occurring on an almost daily basis. Sarah was definitely unsure of exactly how she would respond if these claims were in fact genuine and she came face to face with something evil whilst there. She had gone to Paul, their psychic medium, with her fears and concerns in the hope that he would be able to put her mind at rest.

Paul had been great to begin with. He had sat down with her and waited patiently, listening to everything that she told him. Paul had sat still, thinking to himself for a few moments and then had done his best to explain things to her and put her mind at rest.

"Sarah, listen to me," he had said, taking her small hand in his. "From what you have told me about this case, I will admit this does indeed sound like it is a most disturbed, and perhaps even tragic place. I cannot say for sure until I have had a chance to drink upon the energy of the place but it seems to be an area that knows no rest, by that and reading the report that Andrew prepared on the area around this place, I mean that it is very active.

"Bad things have clearly happened here and may well still be happening. The spirits that linger have found no peace in their passing or the afterlife. So my dear, that will be our number one priority; we will find the source of their pains and sufferings and give them the peace they need."

Sarah had just sat and stared at Paul as if he had just grown a second head.

"But how though, how can we possibly give them peace? What if they are truly evil and do not want or have no need of peace? Hell, they might even enjoy what they are doing to this family. They really might mean to harm them."

Paul had smiled calmly at her, almost patronisingly.

"Sarah," he said, shaking his head slightly. "Firstly, I must ask you, please do not to use that word. Hell is a bad word in and of itself and I will not have it used."

Sarah had to put her free hand over her mouth to hide a slight grin, wondering how he would react to real swear words. The hand hiding her grin must have worked because Paul went on, oblivious to her reaction.

"The distinction that you make, assuming that whatever or whoever is there could be evil, is wrong. There is no such thing as an evil entity or spirit, just lost or misunderstood. Even people who were truly evil in life may still indeed harbour ill to the living, but the nature of spirits do not have the capability of evilness, only mischief or in some extreme circumstances, they have the ability to bully, but they are a pale shadow of who they were. Thus, they lose the capability of any evilness.

"Now let me tell you what I suspect is happening there and what my initial thoughts of these spirits are. Firstly, this disfigured man in the mirror. Andrew has found nothing on him as yet. Why though should we assume him bad? Because he is ugly? Goodness, if that was the case and you were convicted of being evil because you were ugly then I would hazard a guess that this world is full of evil people, living evil people.

"I will not comment on this person or his intent until I see the mirror and can talk to him and find out why he is there. We will have to understand him when we get there, not judge him beforehand. The incidents that have happened in the bathtub firmly suggest a case of murder most foul to me; this is not a harmless spirit. But it could be locked in a loop, killing over and over without even realising it and Mrs Phillips might just be in the wrong place at the wrong time. Unfortunate I know, but very possible."

Sarah was having a hard time trying to digest what Paul was saying; she was not at all convinced that she agreed with him so she sat nodding whilst listening. She saw her chance and thought to catch him off guard.

"Okay, that's a fair comment, Paul, but didn't you say 'that could mean her harm'? Is that not evil actions? What about the bathtub full of blood that Mrs Phillips has seen on several occasions?"

"Well, obviously, as I stated they can bully, but it is possible that this spirit does not even know she is there. As to the bathtub being full of blood, I cannot explain that," Paul said, his tone was almost one of boredom. "Maybe it is the poor woman's mind playing tricks on her, maybe she is making that part up for attention."

Sarah pulled her hand back from Paul angrily at his flippant comment. He continued anyway.

"As for this stabbing in the sitting room, I believe that is almost certainly residual energies. Whatever happened is simply just repeating itself."

"Sorry, Paul, you lost me. Residual?"

"Residual energy, my dear, is the term we use to describe, how can I put this? Yes, spiritual entities that have no intelligence. There are different types of spirits or energies. Intelligent spirits are entities that are aware of themselves, they know who and what they are and are aware of everything that they do.

"Unintelligent entities or residual energies are mere impressions of what once was. They are the leftover spirits of beings doomed to repeat their actions and deeds over and over with no knowledge of themselves. They do not know anything; they just are and do."

Sarah was desperately trying to follow Paul's words and take in and understand what he was telling her, but it was definitely confusing. She had asked Paul about the daughter's bedroom and surprisingly, he had dismissed that as the ramblings of a teenage girl seeking attention after her parents' experiences and refused to comment further on it until he had assessed the room for himself.

That comment had stung Sarah badly, having experienced that sort of blind prejudice herself for years when she was younger. She would have almost understood and expected that type of comment from Andrew, who would have made it purely to wind her up, but coming from someone like Paul, whose whole career was based on people's beliefs, seemed somewhat strange and uncalled for.

Thinking of Andrew had made Sarah smile; the dynamics that she had been witness to between Andrew and his younger sister Jessica were just fantastic. Having invited Andrew and Jessica over for coffee to discuss the case yesterday had proved interesting, to say the least. Tom was there with them as well and they had sat in the kitchen around the dining table discussing it.

Sarah had started by telling them again about the request for help she had received and let them read copies of the emails from Susan Phillips that she had printed off for them. Andrew had read the 'supposed hauntings' as he had called them and laughed. This was not the wisest of moves in Jessica's presence. She had leaned forwards, putting her elbows on the table and glared at her brother.

"You just will not accept anything, will you? Just because you strut around with your head lodged firmly up your own arse and your eyes shut to the possibilities all the time, it does not mean that the rest of us should as well."

"Really, Jess? Really, I mean come on, have you read this shit? I mean, look here." He pointed at his sheet of paper. "A bath full of blood; like hell, maybe she was on her period or something." That got the desired reaction from her.

"You're such a prick, Andy. Honestly, is that your answer to everything? Time of the month! It's always the bloody same with you. You're an asshole, don't ya think it's time you stopped talking complete bollocks and come and join the rest of us in our century."

"Okay, okay." He grinned at her, holding his hands up in surrender. "But here's a thought for you though, sis, maybe she gets abused by her husband and made this shit up. No, come on, don't look at me like that, Jess, you hear it all the time. Women like to protect their men, even though they know that they will still get beaten."

"No, you're absolutely right," Jessica smirked sarcastically. "I have heard it so often. 'No, my husband hasn't hit me, it was this ghost that pushed me down the stairs.' Get real, you stupid idiot."

It had gone on like this for a while. Tom, Sarah was sure, loved to sit and watch the two of them fight the way they did. Eventually, Sarah had to force them into a truce and ask them to agree to disagree on the subject to which

Andrew got in the last shot by saying, "Well, Sarah, I would agree with my little sister but then we would both be wrong."

Sarah just shook her head as Jessica sat fuming at her brother's pig-headedness. They agreed to spend the Wednesday researching anything that they could find on the area and have it ready for Thursday evening when they were going to Dorset.

By the end of the evening, all was calm, the siblings had even come to an agreement of sorts, they were both going to prove the other wrong and accept a forfeit if they lost.

Jessica had promised to prove Andrew wrong and when she did, she would buy him an 'I believe in ghosts' T-shirt. In return and by stating that he was no chauvinist, he told her that she could do his washing for a year when he proved it all for what it really was—rubbish. They left Sarah and Tom at about half past eleven, Andrew promising to find them something to go on and Jessica mumbling about her brother being a male chauvinistic bastard whilst enquiring after his shirt size.

Sarah couldn't help but smile as she thought about the group that she and Tom had managed to gather about themselves. As she looked out through the window at the darkness outside, she asked Tom, "Where are we, love?"

"Just coming up on Yeovil, we should be at our hotel in half hour or so. Then it's straight off to bed for me and a look around the town tomorrow before we meet the Phillips tomorrow afternoon. When is the all-knowing one arriving?"

She tried not to laugh and said, "He said that he was going to catch the train down tomorrow; said he needed the quiet to prepare himself. He did want to do the walk around with us, but I said no, that we wanted to do it ourselves without any distractions. I think, to tell you the truth, he took it personally, so now he's sulking. He said that he should arrive about lunch time, I even offered to pick him up from the train station but he refused saying that he did not want to impose, and would get a taxi to the hotel."

"You gotta really feel for the driver, don't you?" Andrew's voice came from the back. Jessica punched him lightly on the arm but still laughed herself.

Sarah looked out the window again at the lights flashing by in the dark. It wouldn't be long before they reached Dorchester and their hotel.

"Hey guys," Tom said, looking over his shoulder, "do you want to give us a brief rundown of what you found out about the place before we get there?"

"Sure, why not," Jessica replied.

Andrew started it off. "Okay, guys, so this is the bare bones of what we found. Our clients, the Phillips, live in a small village just outside of the town of Dorchester. Now, this village is only about ten years old, so rather than concentrating on just the house, which would have proved useless, we looked at the whole village."

Andrew checked his papers, "The village is called Castleleigh, named after some old lord who owned the lands a few hundred years ago. I'll get to that in a minute. Anyhow, some rich developer bought the land about seventeen years ago and has developed this village and so made himself a tidy little profit, or more accurately, a bloody fortune. Here's the deal; back when this lord, hang on, I got his name somewhere." Andrew shuffled through his papers.

"Oh, here it is, a Lord Robert Castleleigh. Anyway, back when Lord Robert owned this land in 1748, some really bad shit happened. The details are a bit sketchy after all these years, but this is what we have been able to find and put together. From what we understand, one of his servants went a bit loopy and murdered Robert's wife; as the stories go, he hacked her to pieces with an axe, and then tried to kill the daughter.

"Apparently, Robert caught him in the act and, in what was described as self-defence, killed the worker. Being who he was, nobody questioned his actions. We could not find any records of where the wife was buried, we presume somewhere on the lands. That was the end of that, so all was okay in the lord's home again."

Sarah gave a small shiver, not totally certain if it was from the cold or not.

"It gets better," Andrew continued. "A year or so later, some pissed off servant, my theory is a lover of the worker who was killed, took an axe to the lord and his daughter both. At her trial, she claimed that she was innocent; aren't they all? And claimed that there were other men there in the house that had killed the lord and his daughter. She was promptly found guilty and hung for her crimes."

"Was it her?" Tom asked. "Or was it someone else?"

Jessica took up the tale. "Who knows, the records are sketchy at best, we may never know. The really weird thing though is that the bodies had been missing parts."

"Parts? Like what?"

"Well, Tom, Robert Castleleigh's body had no hands and his daughter had no head. The missing parts were apparently never found. The maid denied any knowledge of their whereabouts."

Sarah now knew her shivers were not from the cold.

"After all that," Jessica continued, "the place was inherited by some relative who had it for quite a few years. There is some mention of witchcraft and satanic rituals, missing persons and someone called Constance. There were some unproven accusations of fraternisation with the staff, but apart from that, nothing else of substance. Or at least, nothing we could find. Afterwards, it was pretty much abandoned, and it was left to go to ruin. From time to time, travellers or such would arrive and set up camps on the lands and I'm sure that a few crimes would have been committed, but if there were, we couldn't find any evidence of it. Just a side comment, the old Castleleigh home is now owned by someone who is renovating it as a guest house, A Lucy Edwards. She has changed the name to Castle Gate for all the good that will do if it really is haunted – good luck to her, I think she might need it. Maybe if we find anything relating to Castleleigh, we could pay this Lucy a visit and have a look around the old house? Might help answer some questions and shed a light on things. Plus, Paul would love it at an old mansion."

Half turned in her seat and glancing over at Andrew and Jessica, Sarah asked, "Well, that kind of falls in with some of what Mrs Phillips said, but only vaguely. Is it possible that this Robert Castleleigh character is the one who shows Alice Phillips his bloody stumps? I like your idea of having a look at his former home, we'll see if we can make time. I did get your sarcasm, Andrew, but I do think Paul could learn a lot of the history there. Did you find anything else?"

Andrew laughed. "Did we? Oh yeah, we did. Let me answer your other question first though.

"Yes, Jess and I both think that if, and I do say if, the place is haunted, then it could well be this old lord. Why he is there, though, is beyond us; he was killed in his own house a way away. Why he doesn't haunt his own place is a mystery. Again, a visit to his old home could prove useful. But I do have to say, and you know I'm a sceptic, Sarah, if we could find these records of the murders, others could as well. And just as easily. Please bear that in mind before you jump to believe everything that you've been told by these people."

Sarah gave him a nod whilst Jessica rolled her eyes and shrugged at her brother. Andrew continued, "Quite a few years later, 1834 to be precise, a big house stood on what would have been the edge of the lands previously owned by Robert Castleigh. This house was owned by a gentleman by the name of Jon Farrow. This house was the scene of some very weird and twisted shit, guys.

"Again, records are not complete and there are a few theories. Let me tell you the facts as we have them, then we will tell you what me and Jess think happened."

"Go on," Sarah urged.

"Jon Farrow, the house owner, was away on business, he was a banker. He had gone away and left his wife Emily alone in their home. I have no idea why, but for some reason, Emily did not take her husband's name when they married, he took hers. Anyway, Emily did have a sister and she stayed with her when Jon was away. Emily would always get nervous when left on her own, according to a statement taken from Jon Farrow.

"This sister, Julia—man, she was a really twisted bitch—but I will explain what I mean in a minute, here is what happened. In the basement where it all happened, Emily had been found naked, she had been beaten and her body viciously disfigured by a large knife. There was another man in the house, also naked and disfigured by, what the police at the time believed, the same knife. There are no records on this poor man and no one knew exactly who he was. Julia the sister was also found dead, she had been stabbed as well."

"Okay, go on, Andy, let's have it, what's your theory?"

"Ah, all in good time, my good Thomas. The reports tell us that the police believed the sister, Julia, went mad and killed her own sister and this mysterious unknown gentleman too, and then, lost in her own mad grief, she cracked and took her own life."

"Right, but you think?"

"Now we get to it. See, me and Jess think that there were actually four people there involved in the murders."

Sarah said, "Come on, Sherlock, out with it."

"Jess?"

"Thank you, big brother; okay, here is what we think happened. Julia killed Emily Farrow and this other gentleman, who knows why, but come on, why kill yourself afterwards? Besides, we think it was Jon Farrow that was the fourth person, that he came home, found Julia in the process or the aftermath of killing them and killed her. She was the only one who was still fully clothed and dead. Jon supposedly returned the next day, but we reckon he arrived in the night when this was going on. We think it was definitely Julia who killed the two and Jon who did for Julia, because, as I said, she was still clothed. Anyway, like we say, it's only our theory, all we really know for sure is that Emily and Julia Farrow and the unknown gentleman died on the site that night."

"Alright," Tom said, "the enigma is definitely the unknown guy; you can't find any clue to whom he was?"

"No," Andrew replied. "He could have been a friend or a lover, of which sister we don't have the foggiest. Hell, he could have just been a lover of both of them or just some poor guy who got in the way of a sibling rivalry. So, that is just about it."

"Jesus, this is getting serious. Is that everything you guys managed to find? Please tell me it is because that is certainly more than enough weirdness for me."

"Sorry, Tom, old buddy." Andrew grinned. "But there is more. Go on, Jess, you can have the honours of this one."

"Right then, let's come bang up to date, well, almost. Back in 2001, when people first started moving into Castleleigh, there was one family in particular we found who couldn't fail but to stand out.

"Mr and Mrs Thompson. They moved into the village with their two young children—Peter who was four and Stacey who was just one."

"Oh god, I don't like the sound of this," Sarah said.

Jessica continued, "Because of how recent it was, we were able to get our hands on literally loads of information about what happened. Don't worry, Sarah, I will just give you the basics, I have printouts if you want to read any more."

Sarah turned to face the front, staring out at the road ahead as she wrapped her arms, covered in goose bumps, protectively around herself.

"Mrs Thompson, Catherine, was by all accounts a manic depressant. She had seen loads of doctors and shrinks and was on enough medication to make her rattle if she jumped about too much. Her husband, Oliver, was away a lot. He worked and was often away from home for days at a time. The report states that person or persons unknown broke into the house and murdered Mrs Thompson and the two children. Details of the murders are sketchy but it is believed that after the killings happened, the perpetrators stayed in the house waiting for the husband, Oliver Thompson.

"When he arrived home, they killed him and set about torching the house. It burned pretty much all evidence away so the killers were never caught. Forensics had a nightmare at the scene and was able to discover very little. We however think that there must be more to it than simple murder and arson.

"I mean, why this family? Why the whole family, including the children? Could Oliver have been involved in something shady? I reckon he may have pissed off the wrong people and the murders were a hit. I'm convinced the police know more than they let on and put in the reports, but we have no way to prove it. The records we have are pictures, reports and forensic findings."

Jess looked at her brother for support, not sure if Sarah was even listening anymore or not.

"As Jess said, there is a lot more detail in the reports, so if you want to read them, let me know and I can give you a copy."

"Jesus Christ," Sarah sobbed. "Why the hell would I want to read any more about these sick bastards? Just what the hell is wrong with these people? Why the children? Why?"

Jessica leaned forwards, putting her hands, in an effort to comfort her friend, on Sarah's shoulders. "I don't know, hun, I really don't. Look, there is one more case to tell you about. Shall we just leave it though and wait until the morning?"

"No," Sarah gently shook her head, lifting her left hand up to her right shoulder and holding Jessica's hand, rubbing gently with her thumb. "Let's just have it. It's what we are here for, after all. Let's just get it done, okay."

Andrew nodded. "Okay, the last one then, this guy makes the others look like real saints. Evidence and reports, pictures and news reports, both paper and television, are found in abundance for this guy. He was a real piece of scum, some real evil twisted and sick bastard who went by the name of James Pembleton."

* * * * *

Paul checked his watch as the train pulled into the station Just after twelve noon. *Typical, no damn taxis as usual,* Paul thought to himself as he got off the train and glanced across at the taxi rank from the platform. He did however spot a welcome sight, a coffee stand just outside of the station. *Frères coffee,* he read the sign; *it had better be an improvement on the crap they served on the train,* Paul thought. *Might as well have a cup while I wait for a taxi.*

Paul walked over to the coffee stand and read the surfboard menu, deciding what to have. The black van stood with its back open under the gazebo. Paul looked from the menu to the two men sat in their deck chairs and cleared his throat.

Toby jumped to his feet. "Hi there, what can I get you?"

"Can I have a cappuccino please?"

Toby turned his back and began to make Paul his coffee. Kit looked up at him and smiled. "So, what brings you to Dorchester?"

Paul looked at Kit and smiled, then leant to one side and looked, squinting over Kit's shoulder into the back of the gazebo next to where Toby was working.

Interesting. "Well, let me see, I'm here to investigate some supposed hauntings."

"Oh wow, that's like well cool. So are there many ghosts here?"

Toby finished making the coffee and handed it to Paul. "There you go, that's two pounds please. Help yourself to sugar."

Paul fished around in his pocket and found some coins, paid him then returned to the question. "Thank you, hmmm," he said, sipping his drink. "That's lovely. Are there many ghosts? Tell me Kit, do you believe in ghosts?"

"Nah, personally I think there is no such thing, like, well, I have never seen anything to make me believe. Hang on, do I know you? How did you know my name?"

"Your friend there told me."

Toby laughed, clapping quietly. "No, I didn't."

"No…Ah, Toby. No, I am quite aware that you did not. It was your ever-present guest, it was him." Paul pointed behind the two towards the back of the gazebo where he been looking.

Kit looked behind. "Yeah whatever. Great trick. I love it, but really, come on, how did you know?"

"Why do non-believers always mock and yet seek the most answers? This man is always with you whilst you are here in this place. He sits with you on your chairs and he stands watching you. He shares your laughs and your sorrows, your hopes and dreams. He understands and loves your fears. He waits patiently for his opportunity, he wants to tear your souls from your dead bodies, but you must not let him."

Toby looked behind him too. "Hey look, it's our invisible ghost. Seriously though, who the hell in their right mind would want to haunt a coffee stand?"

"Let me ask you boys a question. What was here before? He knows, oh yes, he knows, for he was here. He teases you both, he laughs at you. Do you or have you ever felt that you are not alone? Do you ever see something from the corner of your eye, some movement that catches your attention but nothing is there when you turn to look? Do you ever feel suffocated? That is what he wants; yes, I can see it now. He wants you on your own. He wants to hold you down and trap you forever, he wants you with him."

"Oh wow," Kit grinned. "It must be my lucky day, a gay ghost." Toby laughed.

"I do not joke, gentlemen, nor do I like being accused of telling untruths. Please, do not take what I have told you lightly, he is here, now, watching you. He follows you everywhere and he knows your secrets. You have been judged by him and when you go, he will be waiting for you. Then he will destroy your souls."

"Fuck yeah," Kit grinned. "A gay ghost who watches me and wants me. How lucky am I?"

Toby joined in. "So, are we damned? Is that what you're saying? Or just fucked?"

"I only tell it as it is, he wants his hands upon your throats, he wants to feel your life as it leaves your bodies. Be sure, he has been here before and will be again. Aahh, look, a taxi, and well, I must be going. That coffee was most delicious, I thank you." Paul dropped the empty cup into the bin, picked up his case and crossed the road towards the waiting taxi. Stopping, he turned back and called, "Give my best regards to Mr Pembleton." Then he was at the taxi.

Toby turned to Kit. "What a complete fucking weirdo."

Kit sat back down in his chair, watching as Paul walked away. He closed his eyes and it hit him. Kit opened his eyes, he was flat on his back, sinking slowly through the yielding wet, soft and cold concrete, and he could feel it seeping through his clothes as he grew heavy, cold and wet.

Big and strong calloused hands held him tight by the throat, pushing him down, forcing him down until he could feel the wet runny concrete begin to enter his ears and as his head sank lower, it began to enter his nose and mouth.

His eyes stared out in panic as the concrete came rushing up and into his eyes, filling them and agonisingly burning through his vision until he could no longer see anything but a white-hot pain and was blind. He could not see, nor could he speak for the concrete slowly slipping down past his tongue and filling his throat.

Kit's hands grabbed blindly for the wrists holding him, trying desperately to tear them away from him; it was no good. The hands were just too strong for him. Suffocating darkness was coming down to join the panic as his strength to fight fled from him and disappeared. Death came to claim Kit as the will to live left him and he succumbed to his cold, wet and terrifying end. He could struggle no more, as he realised that he was dead.

Toby turned back to the van as something hit him and he was forced backwards. Rough calloused hands held him down in the dirt. One hand went away but the enormous strength of the remaining hand held him firm as the other grabbed vast handfuls of dirt and forced it into his mouth, past his tongue and down his throat. A choked half scream crossed his gritty lips as the rough dirt was forced past his lips whilst more was being ground roughly into his eyes, scratching his eyeballs to a pulp, blinding him in agony. More and more dirt was forced down his throat.

Toby couldn't breathe, he thrashed about, his arms reaching but not able to find the strong hands holding him down, his legs kicking out in a feeble attempt to move. The weight on him was getting greater whilst the pressure on his throat grew less. Toby felt like he was being punched all over his body. With his eyes gone, he did not know that the punches were spade loads of dirt landing on him and the pressure as he was being slowly buried alive. He tried and tried to struggle until he had no strength left in him.

Toby could no longer lift his arms or legs against the weight of the dirt piled on top of his body. The weight was too much to be able to struggle against or attempt to breathe anymore. Toby neither saw nor felt anything else, his life had abandoned him, he was dead.

Kit opened his eyes, jumped up from his chair and froze as he and a shaken Toby spotted the spilt coffee beans all over the floor. Someone had used their finger to write in the coffee: 'James Pembleton is watching you'. The sudden rising wind blew through the gazebo, taking the spilt coffee with it.

Toby fell back into his chair beside Kit as he too sat back down, they both sat rubbing their sore and bruised throats whilst blinking furiously at the stinging sensations that they could both feel in their eyes, too shocked to talk. They watched as Paul waved to them from the backseat of the taxi as it drove past and left them and the train station.

"The Dragon's Arms Hotel, it's on the high street I believe, if you would be so kind, driver," Paul said through the window to the taxi driver.

"Great," the driver said.

"I'm sorry, I do apologise. Is there a problem?"

"No, not at all, it's only two minutes across town. Here, let's put your case in the boot."

The driver got out and opened the car boot putting the man's case inside. *If I gotta do these shit jobs, at least I can bag him twenty pence on the extras*, the driver thought.

As they drove off, the taxi driver looked over to the coffee lads; normally, he would put his hand or thumbs up at them, but he frowned as he saw the stunned look on their pale faces and the big guy standing behind them with his huge and filthy hands resting upon their shoulders.

Pulling up outside the hotel, Paul paid his fare and asked for a receipt. The driver mumbled something under his breath about a tip and a tight bastard.

Paul smiled to himself as he told the driver that he may need a taxi again and asked his name so he could request him. "Gary," the driver said begrudgingly.

"Thank you, Gary, you have been most helpful and kind to me. I would like to see you again; maybe if possible, we can discuss the passenger you constantly carry around with you in the backseat."

Gary smiled both politely and in confusion as Paul turned from the car, climbed the steps and disappeared as he entered the hotel.

Twat, he thought to himself, feeling a slight chill on his neck. He drove off, heading back towards the train station, looking repeatedly in his rear-view mirror. *What passenger?*

"Paul, you made it at last, my friend. Good journey?"

Paul could not stand Andrew but he made the obligatory effort to be nice as he shook the man's hand and made the necessary small talk as the others came over from the bar. It took nearly an hour for Sarah and Tom to bore him whilst outlining their plan. Paul did not hear most of it as he could not stop thinking about the name Pembleton.

It shocked him and shook him even more when he read the report that Andrew and Jessica had prepared and saw that very same name in print. He decided it best to keep it to himself for now though. Sarah and Tom were off to meet the Phillips at about three o'clock and have a walk around their home. After they got back and reported what they had learned, they would all head off to the house and get set up, ready for the coming night's investigation.

Chapter 6
Catherine and Oliver

"I will do my best to be home before dark, love, okay? Please don't fret; it's only a couple of hours' drive. I promise I will be back soon, as quick as I can. Okay, I love you too. Bye darling."

Oliver pressed the end call button on his mobile phone as he started the car. He drove out of his client's driveway heading for home, heading home to his wife Catherine and his beautiful children, Peter and Stacey. Putting his foot down, he could not wait to see them again. He was a bit worried though; the doctors had said that Catherine would be okay, that she just needed a bit of understanding and patience.

Post-natal stress was apparently quite a common condition, but since Stacey had been born just over a year ago, Catherine had really changed, she had gone into herself. She would shout and scream at him or the children for no apparent reason. She would cry and lash out at Oliver. The last year had been a real nightmare for him so he had buried himself in his work away from her whenever possible, just hoping things would get better unaided.

They didn't.

Eventually, they had both agreed that she should see someone and get some help. Was he selfish for not wanting to be at home? Maybe sometimes, yes, but it was so hard for him to see his wife like she was and he was finding it increasingly harder and harder to refrain from lashing back out at her, either verbally or physically. Catherine had help, people understood her condition, while nobody diagnosed or understood the husband's side of things. So he drove home, full of longing and apprehension in equal measures.

Catherine hung up, put the phone down and smiled contently. She was having a good day, the children were behaving, Oliver was coming home and she was calm and happy. Sometimes, she would almost forget how it felt to be happy and to be part of a loving family. She could feel so isolated, so misunderstood and alone. It seemed sometimes that no one understood her or wanted her.

"Mummy!" The call came from the top of the stairs so she rushed out to the bottom of the stairs to see what Peter wanted; hopefully, she could catch him before he shouted again and woke his little sister, Stacey, who was having her afternoon nap. Making it to the stairs in record time, Catherine looked up at her small son looking down at her over the stair gate and a smile danced across her lips to see her handsome little man.

"What is it, sweetheart?" she called up gently.

"Can I come and paint a picture, Mummy?"

"Um, well, go on then, just so long as mummy gets a nice big cuddle and a kiss first."

Peter grinned from ear to ear as he struggled with the catch on the stair gate, screwed his face up in concentration. He rattled it and finally lifted it open. With one hand on the banister, he came down eagerly, jumping off the last stair and up into his mother's arms, giving her the biggest kisses that he could whilst getting swirled around and kissed back.

Flushed and happy, Catherine planted Peter back on his feet and made her way through to the dining room, her little man trailing behind her. She went to the cupboard and crouched down, opening the door and getting out the paper and paints, brushes and the water cup. She put them down on the table, fetched an old newspaper and spread it out so to protect the table from Peter's paint. Filling up the water cup from the tap, she placed it on the table besides the paint palette.

"Come on then." She smiled at Peter, pulling out the chair so that he could climb on. Once he got up, she eased the chair back in so he was close to the table. "Now you have fun, darling, Mummy has to start the tea so we can all eat when Daddy gets home."

"Okay, Mummy, I will paint a picture for Daddy."

"That will be lovely, dear," she said as she walked from the room; she paused and listened at the bottom of the stairs to make sure Stacey was still asleep. Satisfied that she could hear nothing, she went to the kitchen to start the preparations for the evening meal.

"Mummy," came the call from the other room.

"Mummy's busy, honey," she called back.

"Mummy, I need you."

Just two minutes, is it too much to ask? "Just a minute please, Peter, I'm busy."

"Mummy, now, I need help."

"Damn it," she said, her voice was beginning to raise in volume. *Just leave me alone, please.*

"Mummy, now!" the boy shouted.

Catherine was pulling a plate from the cupboard and Peter's shout made her jump; she dropped the plate and watched in horror as it fell from her hands and shattered into pieces on the floor at her feet.

"Peter, wait, damn it," she screamed.

He wouldn't wait.

"Mummy, Mummy now, I need help," he whined.

"Waaahhhh." The baby upstairs had started to cry.

Catherine looked to the door, up at the ceiling and down at the pieces of broken plate scattered across the floor. She could not take this anymore as she broke down, shaking, and began to cry. Peter continued to shout; Stacey continued to cry. Catherine's legs buckled and she sat on the floor with her head in her hands, tears rolling down her cheeks, rocking backwards and forwards. Still Peter called. Still Stacey cried. *Please stop, please. The noise, I can't take it. Shut up, shut up.* "Shut up."

Catherine climbed slowly to her feet, her face a mask of pain and confusion as she stalked back to the dining room to see little Peter sat staring up at her.

"Oh, Mummy, I—"

She grabbed him by the head and threw him to the floor. He screamed and cried in fright as much as pain until Catherine sat down on the floor next to him and lifted his head up by the hair. She smashed it down against the floor over and over until the noise had stopped and his head was nothing but a mess of red, bone and pulp. Finally, he had stopped screaming his noise at her but she could still hear it shooting and throbbing through her head. She continued to smash what was left of his small broken head against the floor, but no matter how many times she did, she could still hear the crying.

Stop it, shut up, and stop it please, please, please. Releasing the smashed mess in her hands, she looked up at the ceiling. *It's up there, the noise, I can hear it. I can stop it.*

Unconsciously and without thought, Catherine wiped the scarlet mess from her fingers down her blouse and got to her feet, turned and walked out through the door. She reached the bottom of the staircase and began her assent up towards the noise.

Catherine stood at the door to Stacey's little bedroom. She could see the child standing in her cot, her arms held stretched out, groping towards her mummy, her face red with tear-streaked cheeks.

Catherine could hear the noise and knew that it had to stop, that she had to stop it. She knew that everything would be alright if she could just make the noise stop. *Noise, so much, not long now. It will be peaceful and quiet for when he comes home. Yes, I will make it nice and quiet for him.*

Catherine walked to the cot, reaching past the child, she bent, picked up the pillow that her baby was standing on, causing Stacey to fall over and for the crying to get even louder.

"Shut up. Why can't you just shut up?" Catherine screamed at the baby.

She pushed the pillow down over her baby girl's head, she leant on it hard. She leant on it until the baby stopped squirming, until the noise finally stopped and it was peaceful. She leant on it until she could hear nothing but the quiet. *Too quiet, it's too quiet. Why, why, the quiet is deafening me.*

Catherine stumbled and sat on the floor with her back up against Stacey's cot. Her head hung down with her hands pressed tightly against her ears, trying to block out the deafening oppressive silence that was overwhelming and pressing down upon her.

The key turned in the lock and the front door opened. The house was all in darkness as Oliver walked through the front door and into the hallway. "I'm back," Oliver called out through the darkness. "Sorry I'm so late; the bloody traffic was a nightmare. Hey, where is everybody? Why is it so dark in here?"

Oliver entered the kitchen and switched on the light, he glanced about but still nobody was to be seen. He could smell something strange, a coppery smell mixed with something else, and some foul odour a cross between rotten flowers and a toilet that hadn't been flushed.

Going back out to the hall, he made his way slowly and cautiously, slightly uncertainly, to the dining room. As he entered, the smell hit him like a solid wall, it became almost overpowering. It went straight up his nostrils and clung to his senses; he could almost taste the appalling odour on his tongue. He stumbled slightly when his foot hit something on the floor.

"What the hell?" he said. Damn kids leaving stuff lying around again. He had lost count how many times he had had to tell Peter to tidy his toys away after he had finished playing with them. Reaching for the light switch on the wall, he blinked at the sudden brightness.

He took in his surroundings, fixing his stare on the bloody thing lying on the floor at his feet and collapsed to his knees in horror as he saw the broken, smashed and bloody thing on the floor that had been his son. Oliver managed to turn his head away just in time as he heaved and emptied the entire contents of his stomach on the dining room floor next to his son.

Tears were streaming down his face and sobs were wracking him as he wiped his face and slid his hands under the body and pulled the boy tightly to himself and sat still for many minutes, hugging Peter securely and protectively against himself, running his hand over Peter's ruptured head.

Why, who? These were the only thoughts that entered and were recognised in his distressed and confused mind.

A sound from upstairs startled Oliver and brought him around, back to his senses. He tenderly laid his son back on the floor and rose to his feet, bloodstained and shaking from head to feet. Oliver clutched desperately at walls and work surfaces, anything to help him stay upright as he made his way through to the hallway and the bottom of the staircase.

Holding the banister tightly, he put his right foot on the first stair, followed by his left and slowly, so slowly, began to climb. Hand foot, hand foot, one after the other as he rose higher and higher up the staircase. It was only when he bumped into the child safety gate at the top that he realised he had climbed to the top. Mechanically, he opened the latch and pushed the gate open. Stepping through, Oliver let go of the gate and allowed it to crash closed behind him.

On autopilot, he found himself in Stacey's bedroom, the soft pink walls with the cartoon giraffe border, the numerous soft toys and dolls scattered about the place and her white wooden cot with something beside it. He stood, just staring uncomprehending at the shape until he finally realised what it was. There she sat, his wife, his beautiful wife. She was still, motionless beside little Stacey's cot. He could not see Stacey.

"My baby girl, where? Where is she, Cat?" His eyes were suddenly drawn to the pillow in the cot and the two small legs protruding out from under it. *Oh no, no. Please lord, no; it can't be, please, dear god.*

Oliver reached out and gripped the pillow with shaking hands. He removed it from the cot and let it fall from his fingers to land softly at his feet, as he looked at his beautiful little baby girl, Stacey. She was beautiful, she was peaceful in her soundless sleep, she was lost to him and this life; she was gone.

For the second time, Oliver collapsed to the floor in pure terror and disbelief, all he could see was his son's brutalised and devastated head on his limp body and his daughter's radiant peacefulness. He should check Cat too, he knew. But what if she had left him as well, it was all just too much to comprehend.

Damn the traffic, he thought, if only he had gotten here sooner. Who could, who would do such a thing?

His whole life, everything that he was and cared about lay all around him, dead and gone forever. For hours he just sat there, silent, destroyed and alone. He could not think, he could not understand. Who and why? They were the only two words, the only two questions that went through his head time and time again, over and over. No matter how many times the questions were asked, Oliver never came any closer to the answer.

"Make it stop, please, the noise. I can't stand it."

Oliver's eyes flew open; the daylight streaming through the window was blinding, and the begging of his wife was a sweet sound. *Cat, my sweet Cat, they didn't take you too, oh thank god*. Oliver found himself leaning over and pulling his mumbling wife to him and hugging her tightly, afraid to let go of her in case she should die too and leave him all alone again.

"Cat," he whispered gently in her ear. "Cat, what, what happened, who was it?"

"The noise, it was the noise. But I made it stop, oh yes, I did. It is quiet now, oh so quiet. Can you hear the silence? It was too loud, but I made it stop, yes, yes it's quiet now."

Catherine mumbled and spoke incoherently for a while; Oliver did not understand her wild ramblings as he had gone half mad with grief himself. Catherine spotted the pillow, lying discarded on the soft red carpet. She screamed in panic.

"No, what have you done? Put it back, please put it back now. The noise, the noise will start again if you don't. The noise, I can't take the noise. Please. Please. Please."

She pushed Oliver roughly away from her as she scrambled to her feet; she fell, got back up and fell again; she crawled on all fours. Catherine seized the pillow, picking it up and roughly throwing it back into the cot. Grasping at the bars, she nearly pulled the cot over on top of herself but managed to rise to her feet before it could fall. She pushed the pillow back down over her baby daughter's body.

"There," she declared. "There, it's okay now, it will stay quiet now."

Oliver looked up through blurred, tear-streaked disbelieving eyes at his wife, and comprehension was dawning. He was seeing his wife, really seeing her properly for the first time since he had returned home late the night before. He saw her ragged and broken appearance and he saw the dry blood on her blouse and hands and arms. Suddenly, he knew.

"The blood, whose is it? You? Was it you? Cat…Catherine? Cat, what, what have you done? They were our babies, our babies, Cat," he whispered to his wife, tears filling and overflowing from his eyes.

Oliver started to his feet and he pulled his wife's arm, tugging at her, pulling her up with him and turning her around so he could look in her mad, wide and vacant eyes. They did not see him, they saw nothing. "Did you do this?" he asked as he held her by her shoulders. "Answer me, damn you," he said, shaking her.

She would not answer; she just looked away over his shoulder with a far off look in her eyes. He begged her for answers. He pleaded and shouted and screamed at her. Still no answer. He shook her, gently at first and soon he shook her like a rag doll. Catherine was lifeless and wilted in his arms as he shook her and shook her, harder and harder whilst screaming in her face.

He threw her to the floor hard and scrambled over and on top of her, grasping at her blouse, lifting and banging her back down against the floor, lifting and smashing her down, time and time again. Catherine did not struggle; she was limp and unresponsive in his hands. It was like Catherine was already dead. Oliver let go of her blouse, letting her slump to the floor, her head lolling to the side. He slapped her face once, twice, thrice, more times than he could remember or count, begging her to tell him why, why she would do this to their babies. Wanting to know what was wrong with her and how she could do this thing.

Oliver was exhausted, sweat dripped from his face to mingle with the blood from his son Peter on Catherine's blouse as he sat on her stomach panting, looking down at her battered and bloody ruin of a face. *I did this*, he thought. *This is all my fault. I brought this on us all. I was never here. I was always too busy and I did nothing to help her, and now they're dead. All of them gone. Dead. I am alone. I deserve to be. I deserve to suffer and die as well. They should be laughing and happy, playing and having fun. I should be the one dead. Not them. Not them.*

Slowly, he removed himself from his wife's body, falling to the floor. How long he lay there motionless he did not know.

Finally, in the mid-afternoon, something clicked on in Oliver's head, forcing him to move. Oliver rolled over to his hands and knees and then climbed uncertainly to his feet and walked from the room, not once looking back.

Oliver was like a zombie in his actions and thoughts, he no longer felt or saw, at least not as a normal person would. He no longer had feelings to give or share, he was neither capable of love or hate. He wasn't a man or a husband or a father anymore, he just was. As if in a trance, Oliver opened the safety gate and made his way down the stairs and through to the dining room where Peter was. Peter was there, still, waiting for him. Crouching down beside the boy, Oliver scooped his son up into his arms; he turned and headed back the way he came, up the stairs and into the pink room.

He carefully laid Peter down next to Catherine; his ruined head upon her chest and he grasped her hand, he pulled and draped her arm over Peter in a cuddle as a loving mother would. Oliver turned to face the cot; he bent in and removed the pillow from Stacey's body. He picked her tiny form up and laid her down with her mother too. They lay there all three, mother, son and daughter; sharing one last loving cuddle that they would keep for eternity. Oliver stood and watched his family.

A few hours after darkness had fallen, Oliver put his big overcoat on and left the house, not even closing the front door. He walked down the path, climbed in his car, started it up and drove. He headed for the nearest petrol station. It was a quiet night on the road, which was just as well the way Oliver drove, staring at the white flashes of the centre line as if he were being hypnotised. By some kind of miracle, he did not crash and kill himself but arrived safely at the garage; he pulled in and purchased three green petrol cans from the attendant. For once, he never considered the cost of petrol as he filled the cans. Screwing the lids in place and putting the full cans in the boot, Oliver went to the office and paid, got back in the car and drove home.

If not for the overcoat he wore, the attendant may have seen the blood on Oliver and could have asked questions, which would lead to police involvement. Oliver did not want that; even in his present state, he still knew that much.

Oliver spent nearly half an hour walking backwards and forwards, throwing petrol up the walls of his house and trailing it over the furniture and carpeted floors. He gave a decent covering downstairs and was halfway through the second can by the time he reached the landing at the top of the stairs.

He used the remainder to slosh petrol over the landing, in the bathroom, through Peter's room and in his and Catherine's own room as well. When Oliver returned to Stacey's room, he was unscrewing the last can. He ran a trail of petrol round the floor, in her cot and threw some up the curtains. He drew a circle of petrol around his family. Using the last of the can's contents, he poured some on Catherine, Peter and Stacey and used the last dregs on himself, pouring it over his head and feeling it run down his face, burning his eyes as it soaked him.

Discarding the can, Oliver walked back down the stairs for the last time. Entering the dining room, he removed a box of matches from the sideboard; he scrunched up the newspaper that Oliver had been using whilst he had been doing his painting; turning the box of matches over in his hand, he looked at it through glazed eyes, slowly lifting his arm up until the newspaper was in front of his eyes.

Oliver fumbled with the box as he extracted a single match from it. He struck the match and held the small flame to the paper and lit it. Dropping the burning newspaper and the box of matches, he was nearly halfway out of the room when the flame hit the petrol-soaked floor.

Whoomp!

Fire instantly engulfed the dining room; it ran out and caught up with Oliver before he even made it to the bottom of the stairs. It climbed his legs, danced over his body and set his head alight like a great candle, it happened faster than the time it takes to tell. The whole downstairs was a raging inferno, the staircase a tunnel of dancing orange, red and yellow flame and Oliver a human candle burning brightly right in the middle of it all.

Pain ripped through Oliver as his hair burnt away like a fuse in seconds and his skin blistered, blackened and cracked open under the intense heat. *Upstairs, I must be with them*, were Oliver's only thoughts as he struggled, one stair at a time in a desperate effort to climb and reach his family.

By the time Oliver had made it three quarters of the way up the stairs, he was blind. The flames had consumed his face and melted his eyes, it had burned him blind. He had heard the pop as they burst. Blood and slime flowing in place of tears but drying and burning off instantly. Up, up he climbed, slowly on all fours, one hand then the other to the top of the stairs, he used the safety gate to pull himself upright. Grasping at the red-hot metal in his groping hands before leaning and tumbling over it, leaving half of the remaining flesh from his hands, still burning, on its metal surface as he fell in a heap the other side.

Barely conscious and in more agony than anyone should have been able to be feeling and still be alive, Oliver determinedly crawled onwards and into his little girl's bedroom. He knew where they were, they were in the middle of the room. It would be a funeral pyre that had once been his perfect family. Close, so close. Closer he crawled, leaving more burnt and dripping flesh wherever he put his ruined hands.

In the end, it was too much. No human could or should have endured the pain as long as Oliver did. It was only through sheer will and determination to be with his family that he had made it this far. But in the end, it was not enough, he did not have the strength to join them that one last time. Oliver gasped through burnt vocal cords and collapsed. Oliver had died with his arm stretched; seeking towards his family, his burnt stumps of fingers stopped a mere inch from where his wife lay with his children, waiting for him.

The fire brigade came fast but could not save the house, it was totally destroyed. The police forensic teams did their job as best they could, as did the fire inspectors. The fire had been so intense that very little evidence remained to be examined. The fire inspector ruled arson. The police never found any witnesses that saw the fire started. The bodies were burnt beyond all recognition and had to be identified through dental records.

Chapter 7
2012 – Sarah

They drove slowly into the village of Castleleigh just after ten to three in the afternoon, following the satellite navigation. Tom brought the car to a stop just outside the house where the Phillips family waited for them. Sarah looked out of the car window and across the lawn, spotting the local estate agent's sign staked into the ground that advertised the house 'For Sale'. She looked up at the house as it sat silent, waiting for them. It was totally ordinary, a modern, two-storey property, red brick, tiled roof, driveway, garage and a postage stamp-sized neatly cropped lawn.

"Come on, babe, let's do this," Tom said quietly to Sarah, shaking her leg gently as she continued to stare silently at the most normal and average-looking house.

Finally, Sarah came around and they got out of the car, Tom locking up and walking around to join Sarah on the pavement. He took her by the hand as they began the walk up to the apparently terrifying house.

After hearing the stories surrounding the place, Sarah had expected to have a real feeling of dread mixed with apprehension and fear as she approached, but there was nothing, no feelings like that at all. She felt instead somewhat let down and disappointed, she just hoped that they would not be disappointed when they got inside the property. It just appeared to be a normal house in a normal street in a normal village. Or at least, that was what it seemed. Sometimes though, images can be deceptive and ultimately lure you into a false sense of security.

Feeling totally relaxed and at ease, Sarah reached her hand up and rang the doorbell. Chimes sounded from inside and soon they could hear footsteps approaching the front door from the inside.

Susan Phillips opened the door to greet her visitors; she was forty-one, blonde (with dark roots) and about five foot four tall wearing a navy turtleneck jumper and jeans. She smiled brightly, but somewhat nervously at Tom and Sarah as they stood on her doorstep. She stretched her arm out and shook their hands. First taking Sarah's hand who shook and smiled back pleasantly and then with Tom.

"Hello, you must be Sarah and Tom? I'm Susan; I'm so very pleased to meet you. Will, err, won't you please come inside?"

Susan waved with her arm as Tom and Sarah crossed the threshold and entered the house.

Sarah stopped in the hallway and looked slowly around. She could see rooms off the corridor in front of her, the stairs to her right went straight up.

"Thank you so much for coming," Susan said. "I can't thank you enough. This place has just got us absolutely terrified. We have been staying at a hotel since our email conversation. Alice, my daughter, just refuses to come back and I must say I don't blame her at all. Brandon hates the place; he won't set foot here again either. The place terrifies me but I-I want answers. I need answers, you know? I have to know what's happening here. Can you help me?"

Tom looked at Sarah, as doubt began to creep into his mind; fortunately, Sarah came to his rescue and took charge.

"Mrs Phillips, Susan. If you don't mind, may I call you Susan?"

"Of course, please."

"Okay, well, obviously, we know roughly what happens or has been happening here through what you have already told me in your emails. What would be great is if you could give us a tour around your home, show us the hot spots where you have experienced the activities you told us about and we can go from there."

"Of course, okay, well, seeing as we are downstairs, follow me into the sitting room. I will show you where Brandon witnessed the stabbing."

Susan turned and walked along the hall, turning left into a long room. The sitting room ran the length of the house from front to back, a bay window facing the front street outside and patio doors leading to the garden. Tom entered first after Susan, followed by Sarah.

"So, Susan, is this where Brandon experienced the stabbing?" Tom asked.

"Yes, it is; my husband came home from work to an empty house. I was out shopping with friends and our daughter, Alice, was sleeping over at her friend's house. When he came into this room, Brandon saw a woman bent over a naked man, she was stabbing him over and over.

"Brandon was horrified. He said there was blood everywhere, he was terrified and rooted to the spot for several seconds. Eventually, he shouted at the woman, but she either could not hear him or else she was completely ignoring him. Brandon decided to call the police; unfortunately, as you can see…" Susan gestured to the telephone on the stand. "…the phone is here, which is right next to where the attack was happening. He tried to be silent, but as Brandon approached the phone, the woman stopped.

"She spun around to face him; the blood on her and the knife flying everywhere. Brandon said she looked surprised, shocked to see him and even a bit afraid. He took her hesitation as a sign and ran from the house, pulling his mobile phone from his pocket. Outside, there was no sign of the woman coming after him; he called the police from the front lawn and waited there for them to arrive."

Susan sighed. "As you know, when the police came, they found no evidence of what Brandon claimed to have witnessed; they verbally laid into him, accusing him of wasting police time and threatened to arrest him. Eventually they left, leaving Bran feeling stupid and not just a little scared."

"Okay," Tom said. "Is that everything that happened in here?"

"Yes, it is."

Tom and Sarah exchanged glances, they were both thinking the same thing, the name Farrow. Sarah's thoughts went further, she remembered what Paul had said about residual hauntings. This wasn't that, the woman had apparently noticed Brandon and reacted to him. This did not fit Paul's explanation or definition of residual.

Tom continued, "Right, Susan, lead the way, and show us what else you have going on here."

Susan nodded and led the way from the sitting room, back along the corridor; she started to climb the stairs when Sarah stopped her.

"Um, Susan, not to be rude but is that it? I mean, not that Brandon's experience wasn't bad but what I mean is…has there been any other activity downstairs? The rest is all upstairs?"

"Yes, that's right. Is there a problem?"

"No, not at all; it just strikes me as odd that with so much paranormal activity happening in your home, only the one occurrence has happened downstairs."

"Don't worry about it, love," Tom said. "Paul will probably have an explanation for this." Susan looked at Tom, confused. She didn't want to question him in front of Susan, but she wasn't sure why he had cut her off and been so dismissive.

"Paul is our psychic medium, Susan, he will be here with us tonight and I'm sure he will be able to help answer some of your and our questions."

Susan nodded as she continued to climb the stairs. On the upstairs landing, she doubled back on herself and led Tom and Sarah into the bathroom, pausing at the door and letting them enter before her.

"Tell us everything about this room please, Susan," Sarah said to a pale Susan.

The room obviously affected her state of mind with what she had both witnessed and experienced in the room.

"Okay well, first off, and the most, I don't know, silly? On several occasions, the water in the bath has turned to blood. Sounds silly, I know, and very Hammer Horror, but I swear I have seen it, the problem being that nobody else has. A couple of times I have gone to fetch Brandon to show him the blood in the tub but it's always the same, the bath will be full of steaming water just waiting for me to get in. Bran used to take the mickey out of me until some of the other things started to happen. Let me show you my neck."

Susan pulled the neck of her sweater down in order to show the yellow bruises on her neck. They had faded somewhat, but on close examination, Tom and Sarah could clearly see the finger and thumbprint bruises on her neck. Sarah touched them with the tips of her fingers, tracing the bruises down Susan's neck. The sudden outbreak of goose bumps on Susan's neck caused Sarah to step back.

"Sorry, Susan, but my god. It…it must have been awful."

"I know, yes, it was. Let me tell you what happened." Susan unconsciously folded her arms and started to rub her arms as if she was freezing cold, but the house was anything but cold.

"I had made Brandon run the bath for me because I was just too scared that it would be full of blood again," she said, shaking her head slightly. "He waited with me as I got undressed and got in. He then left me and went downstairs whilst I enjoyed my soak. With the heat of the bath and the quiet of the house, I managed to relax. I lay back with all my worries forgotten, almost at full stretch in the bath, with my head submerged halfway, you know what I mean…when the water fills your ears and all you can hear is the strange echoing of the water lapping at the sides of the bathtub.

"Anyway, there I was, flushed with the heat and fully relaxed. Suddenly, there were these huge hands on my throat squeezing. It didn't register at first but all of a sudden, I was under the water. Soapy water stung my eyes, blinding me as I squeezed them shut tightly; the hands were rough like sandpaper, like someone who works with their hands, not smooth at all but heavily calloused."

Tom and Sarah exchanged knowing glances again.

"He, whoever he was, was just too damn strong for me. He held me down under the water whilst I tugged and scratched at his wrists. My whole body bucked and twisted in the bath, my legs splashing water everywhere as I struggled uselessly against this man. Suddenly, he was gone, the pressure forcing me under was no more. Instead, someone had me under the arms, lifting me out. My head broke the surface and I took a huge gulp of air, I was still blind from the soapy bubbles so it took a second for me to realise that it was Brandon there who was helping me.

"I think I lashed out, hitting him a few times before I realised that I was safe. Brandon said he could hear me banging around from downstairs, and he came up to see me thrashing around like I was having some kind of seizure. He says that he saw no one, but even Brandon got upset when he saw the angry marks this man had left on my neck."

Susan fell quiet, the look of horror and fear on her face suggested to Sarah that she was thinking about that night. Sarah moved in to hug Susan as she spotted a single tear roll from Susan's eye down her cheek.

"What…what do they want with us?"

"I do not know, Susan, but I promise you this, we will do our absolute best to get to the bottom of it and find some answers for you; are you okay to go on?"

Susan nodded, wiping her eyes with the back of her hand. She led them out of the bathroom, down the hall and into her bedroom where she showed Tom and Sarah her dressing table that stood at the foot of her bed, its mirror covered by a blanket draped across it.

"I put this here," Susan stated. "I put it here because of the man in the mirror, he stands watching me, staring. He is horribly disfigured, not like burnt or anything like that, but scarred, like something out of a horror movie. His eyes don't match, they are different colours and face different directions, and his nose is sort of flat and twisted like it has been broken too many times. He only has one ear and his face looks wrecked as if he had been in a bad car accident or something and stitched back together, but wrong; half his teeth are missing and the other half are either deadened black or deeply stained yellow."

"And what exactly has this man done?" Tom asked her.

"Nothing, he just stands staring, almost a lustful stare. I can't, I won't ever look in there again, even with you guys here. I'm sorry, you probably think me silly but I just can't."

Tom shook his head. "No, Susan, I don't think you're silly at all," he said in a calm and soothing voice. "I think you're the victim of something very sinister. Like Sarah said, we will do everything we can to get to the bottom of all this for you and your family."

"Thank you so much." Susan sighed, her shoulders relaxed, thankful that these people weren't treating her like some kind of lunatic. "Now there is just one more place to show you, my daughter, Alice's bedroom, the poor girl has not set foot in there since I first emailed you. Now she will not even enter the house."

Susan led them out of her room and across the hall to her daughter's bedroom. It was a typical teenage girl's bedroom—an unmade bed, littered computer desk, various CDs and books scattered about and JLS and One Direction posters adorning the walls. Susan crossed the room and sat down on the bed, moving a well-loved and creased paperback novel out of her way.

"Alice has awoken twice before to find herself stripped completely naked and tied to the bed, she had tried to scream out for us but couldn't because a rag had been shoved in her mouth. It was only when I came in to wake her that I found her like this. She told me that a man dressed in an old-fashioned suit stood over her, grinning madly at her and holding a whip in his hand. He said things to her that she refuses to tell me or Brandon, this has only happened twice, because after that she says that she has never seen him again."

"That's good though, isn't it, I mean it's terrible that a girl so young has had to have been put through that kind of ordeal, but at least it's stopped."

"Well, Tom, that's the problem, the first time it happened I was convinced that some pervert had broken into our house and…and raped my…my baby."

Sarah sat down with her arm around Susan, looking up at Tom as the woman beside her broke down in tears.

"It's okay, Susan, it's okay now."

Susan again wiped her eyes, sniffing and trying to get herself back under control; the occasional sob and shoulder shake escaped her.

"I'm so sorry; this has just been so awful for us all. I can't take this anymore. We put the house up for sale but with the current economic climate, we have had no interest and we can't afford to stay in hotels forever. What are we going to do?"

"Susan, I can't promise you that everything will be okay after tonight but we will do everything we can to get answers and rid you of these happenings. Now I think it is for the best that you head off back to your hotel and try to relax, get some rest. Tom and I will get the rest of the team and bring them in."

"I…I have to tell you about one more though; a man, he's in this very room every single morning since the well-dressed man vanished."

"Okay."

"Every morning since those two times, no matter what time it is, whenever Alice would wake, she would see this man stood next to her bed with his back to her."

Tom said, "How do you know it wasn't the same man?"

"Because this man was huge, well over six foot tall, not at all like the first man. This man wore scruffy and dirty clothes and never did anything physical to her. But he could somehow sense her; when she would start to sit up in her bed, he would turn around to face her. She said he would smile at her, almost kindly. The first time she saw him, Alice thought that he was almost, I don't know, looking after her? She had smiled back at him until he raised his arms at her. Alice said he had no hands; all there was were bloody stumps where his hands should have been. Every time, every morning, it was the same man and the same strange smile. Every day, he would show her his bloody stumps, it was at that point that she would leap, terrified from her bed, and run into mine and Brandon's room, crying her little heart out. We even tried putting her in the spare room but when she awoke, he would always be there, standing over her."

Sarah stood up. "That's everything, Susan?"

"Yes."

"Okay. I'm going to need your house keys and you're going to go and join your family. You have been wonderful, but you need to rest now. We will take it from here. Tom and I will get the rest of our group in and see what we can sort out for you. Okay?"

"Okay and thank you."

Susan fished in her pocket for her keys; she took her car key from the bunch and handed Sarah the rest.

"Thank you," Susan managed as she stood up and left the room.

Hearing the front door shut and a minute later a car start and drive away, Tom sat down next to Sarah on the bed.

"Well, babe, I hope you're ready because this is one fucked up situation."

Sarah nodded; she knew Tom was tense by his language. But she still had to know. "Tom, what was that about earlier? Downstairs I mean, when I asked Susan about anything else. You cut me off and said basically Paul would deal with it."

Tom sighed, "Listen love, there is some strange shit going on and I just didn't want to burden the woman any further or give her anything else to worry about. I just thought that if I said that about Paul, she wouldn't worry as much. Trust me Sarah, it wasn't intended to belittle you in anyway. I promise. Now give us a hug and let's get out of here."

Sarah moved in and put her arms tightly around Tom, she didn't realise how much she needed that hug until he was holding her. Looking over Tom's shoulder, she looked around the girl's bedroom, Sarah was thinking that she had been so wrong in her assumptions and that there was absolutely nothing normal or average about this normal and average house.

There was nothing left for them to do so Sarah and Tom left the house, locking it up behind them. They drove off to get the rest of the team. It was going to be a long night.

It was nearly half past four when Tom and Sarah met up the rest of the team back at the Dragon's Arms. Andrew was busy in the bar chatting up the young lady working there, much to Jessica's amusement, as the girl rebuked his every advance. Paul was in his room, 'preparing himself' for the night's events.

Leaving Tom with Jessica and Andrew, Sarah headed up to let Paul know it was nearly time to go; reaching the third floor and finding Paul's room 312, Sarah knocked loudly on the door. No answer.

Sarah knocked again. Again, no answer so she banged as loud as she could with her fists. "Yes," said the impatient voice from within the room.

"Paul, it's Sarah. It is nearly time to go, are you ready?"

"I shall be ready soon."

"Okay, but we really want to get set up before it gets dark."

"I said soon."

Idiot. "Tom said we leave at five, anyone not on board gets left behind."

The door opened and Paul's face appeared around the door's edge. "I will be there in two minutes, now leave me."

The door slamming shut in her face, Sarah turned on her heel and headed back to the stairs, thinking she really wasn't sure that having Paul with them was a good idea.

At five o'clock they were ready to go, the car was packed up with their equipment and Paul had sat in, refusing to help with the gear. Jessica, Sarah and Tom had packed the gear; Andrew eventually helped them after finally giving up on the barmaid as a lost cause. Jessica had commented about the girl being over the moon at Andrew's defeat and eternally grateful for them taking him away.

They set off to the sound of Paul advising them on what to expect, insisting that he must be allowed a walkthrough first to get a feel of the atmosphere. He wanted to be prepared and forewarned of what was waiting for them.

At five thirty, they arrived. Sarah entered the property with Paul whilst the others started to get the equipment ready; with time and the fading light against them, Paul and Sarah would only have ten minutes to walk around before the others entered to set up the cameras and sound equipment.

Paul stood in the hallway looking around; he took Sarah by the hand, leading her to the sitting room. He stopped, staring at a particular spot, exactly where Susan had said Brandon witnessed the stabbing. "Yes, this is it. This is where…Wait, what? Yes, that's right." He nodded and spoke as if there were others in the room with them.

Sarah could feel the goosebumps begin to rise.

"Paul, who are you talking to?"

"Sshh, I'm busy. Yes, I know, but do not worry about this one; she is of absolutely no concern to you. You can talk to me. Now tell me please, sir, what is your name?"

Sarah put her hand on Paul's arm. "Paul, who is it?"

Paul turned around to face Sarah, a forced smile struggling to cling to his lips.

"I think you had better go wait with the others, Sarah. He refuses to speak to me whilst you are here in the room."

"No, Paul. I need to know who is here; I need to know what is happening."

"I will fill you in later, now leave me," he snapped, shrugging his arm from her grasp and continued talking to whoever was there.

Shaking her head, Sarah walked dejectedly from the room and outside to join the others. Silently seething, she met Tom by the car and explained to him Paul's behaviour and attitude towards her.

"Don't let him get to you, love, really, he likes to overact and be at the centre of any attention, you know that. Besides, I still don't fully trust the guy and I think any results we can get either with the cameras or recorders will be worth a million times what he can come up with. I mean, with him, we have to take his word on what he says to be the truth. With us, we will have real, hard evidence to work with. And it will be real evidence that can't be discredited."

"I know you're right, he is just so bloody infuriating."

"He does it on purpose, love. He enjoys pushing yours and everyone else's buttons."

"I know, but there's something else, Tom. I don't know, I can't explain it. But what or whoever he was talking to in there wanted me out and so did he. I thought we were a team, he should have told it that I stayed but he didn't. I don't know, call me stupid but it almost seemed like he wanted me out, like whatever it was he was getting, Paul didn't want me to know anything about it."

"Well, the hell with Paul. We will do our investigation our way and get our results. We will go all out to get the answers and help this family, and if Paul gets in my way. Well, let's leave it at that, but he better not interfere where he's not wanted tonight."

Andrew and Jessica were busy setting up the equipment. Andrew had a full report on where the events had happened and a description of the occurrences. Keeping well out of Paul's way, they started in the sitting room. Andrew set up a night vision camera by the window facing towards the 'stabbing area', and put a digital voice recorder on the mantelpiece in order to capture any sounds or voices. He went from room to room setting up similar equipment with Jessica trailing electric cable all over to power the equipment. When they got to the bathroom, Andrew had an idea.

"Right, Jess, if I leave you a camera and recorder, can you fill the bathtub? If things supposedly happen when it's full then it makes sense to do so. I will go and do the parents' room and then the daughter's. See you in a few."

"Okay, Andy, no worries."

Andrew left her to get on with it, putting the camera and recorder on the toilet seat. He walked out to the hallway and into the bedroom of Susan and Brandon

Phillips. He could hear the sound of water filling the bath as he worked. Finishing up, he crossed to Alice's bedroom; unfortunately, Paul was still in there.

"Uh, sorry, Paul, I didn't know you were still here. Look, I need to set this stuff up, I won't be a second, okay?"

"Yes, he is one of them. I had better go now. Yes, William, I will indeed see you later." He got up and left the room without even acknowledging Andrew's presence.

"Twat," Andrew muttered as he set the equipment up.

"What's that you say?"

Andrew looked up at the sound of his sister's voice. "The guy is such a wanker, sis. He ignores me completely whilst pretending to talk to some guy called William."

"Maybe he was," Jessica offered.

"Bullshit. The guy is an arse. Now come on, we better tape all this cable down and test the equipment before we show Tom and Sarah."

As Andrew and Jessica busied themselves, taping and securing the electric cable safely so that in the dark no one would be able to trip over it, Paul sat quietly in the back of the car. He was contemplating everything that he had learned about this place and its residence from William and decided that tonight was going to prove both a very interesting and deadly night.

Once all was done, it was nearly eight o'clock and completely dark. The whole team gathered together by the car so Andrew could explain what he had done.

"Right then, first up, be careful of the cable running throughout the house, it is stuck down but in the dark you never know so just be aware. The cable feeds back out to here where anyone not inside the house can observe those who are from the television on the back seats. Okay, so we have one camera in the lounge, it is pointing where Brandon saw the stabbing and we have a digital voice recorder on the mantelpiece. This way we can see and hear if anything happens in there.

"Upstairs, we have a camera on the sink facing the bath, which incidentally is full of water, and the recorder is next to it. In the parents' room, we have a camera facing the dressing table and the recorder is sat on the dressing table. I have removed the blanket so if anything or anyone appears, we will get it. In the girl's, room we have the recorder on the bed and the camera facing it from her chest of drawers. I think that covers just about everything."

"Okay," Tom said, looking at all the different rooms on the television, "good work, mate, you certainly seem to have covered all the angles. Anything else we need to know?"

"I have two portable hand-held night vision cameras and two digital voice recorders left, so we can go around in two teams and try to interact with whatever is there and capture more evidence of anything else that may happen out of sight of the stationary gear. I'm all set and powered up so we are ready to go when you are."

Sarah nodded. "I think we should sort teams now. Tom, I think you should go in with Andrew first and see what you can turn up. Jess and I can go second. Paul, I think the best thing for now is for you to remain here to advise the investigation and answer any questions."

Paul wasn't too happy about this. He wanted to be inside guiding the night's events to his plan but could not risk pushing his luck yet. "I think I will definitely be of more help if I move between you and give advice and guidance as we go."

Andrew rolled his eyes. "That sounds good and all but I think that from all of the reported events, if there really is anything here, then it will almost certainly favour you girls."

Sarah agreed. "That is true, but it would corroborate anything we find if you guys can come up with something first. So we will see what, if anything, happens for you two and then me and Jess will take over or we can swap around further if we think it necessary. Paul, I really want you here to give suggestions and answer questions. I think it best to save you until things really start happening.

"Anything else, or shall we get this going?" Nobody answered.

Paul smiled knowingly to himself.

Sarah looked at the faces around her as she prepared mentally for the night ahead. Taking a deep breath, she spoke. "Okay then, let's get the lights turned off and start this."

Chapter 8
1998 – James Pembleton

Excerpt from the Daily Echo, 17 July 1998

Police still baffled by the disappearance of seven local women

The police still have no idea on the whereabouts or even the wellbeing of seven young women, still missing from the Dorchester area. Once a week now for the last seven weeks, a young woman out on the town having fun on a Saturday night has gone missing. Tomorrow will be the eighth Saturday in a row. Police have 'significantly increased patrols' around the town in the hope of catching the perpetrator. This suggests to this reporter that they have absolutely no clues as to the identity of the kidnapper. They are however, now willing to admit that the same person is indeed highly likely to be responsible for all of the disappearances.

The first women, Rebecca Deans, disappeared on 30th May this year; she was reported missing by her family the next day.

Each and every week a young woman, each has had approximately the same looks and build about them.

Every girl was a redhead, being about five feet five inches tall and slim built. The perpetrator has targeted this particular type of women; the reasons for this are so far unknown.

Every incident to date, it has now been released, is almost definitely the same person. He or she has posted a cutting of the victim's hair that has been tied into a knot along with her clothes and purse to her home address. But despite the overwhelming evidence, the police are refusing to link these events to other murders with very similar women and series of events from all over the country over the last several years.

Police are advising ANY woman, regardless of how she looks, as it is possible this person's 'tastes' could change, not to go out alone and to always be with a group of friends that she knows and trusts.

We all hope that this sick individual will be caught soon and that the town of Dorchester and the surrounding arrears can relax once more. We can only pray that tomorrow night will be the night that the pattern breaks and our young women will be safe on the streets once again.

He folded the newspaper, tossing it on the table as he picked up the half-drunk pint of lager.

He brought it to his lips and took a huge swallow, before setting it down once more and smiled to himself.

"James, yo James." A young man who he knew from the building site he worked at was making his way over with a pint in each hand. Sitting himself down opposite, the new man placed the glasses on the table, glancing briefly at the newspaper headline as he chucked it onto the table next to him.

"So, me and the lads are getting totally shitfaced tonight down in Weymouth tonight. You up for a night out, James?"

He shook his head. "No."

"Come on, man, it'll be an awesome night, apparently the birds down there are right up for it, if you know what I mean? Easiest lay ever, so whatcha say?"

"No."

"Come on, Jimmy, don't be like that. Steve said the birds are fit as fuck, man. We can get pissed, pull a decent bit of stuff and take them back to their place and shag their brains out. What more do you want on a Saturday night?"

"How about some goddamn peace and fucking quiet, you moron," James said as he got to his feet.

The man looked up at James from his seat. "Sorry, man, what's up? Come on, at least drink the pint I gotcha."

James leaned in close to the man's face and whispered. He whispered so quietly that the man struggled to hear him.

"Listen to me, you stupid little fuck, I am not interested in a night out with you or pulling some local slag. I'm going back to the caravan on site. One more word from you and I will beat you so fucking bad, you won't be capable of even looking at another bitch, let alone doing anything else with it."

The man sat still, he visibly paled as James turned his back and stalked out of the pub.

At precisely nine o'clock that evening, James Pembleton walked through the door of the Royal Acorn pub; he did a quick look around and smiled to himself as he saw the pretty redhead sat up at the bar on her own. Walking to the opposite end, ignoring her, James sat on a stool and waited until the bar man was free and ordered himself a pint of lager.

Over half an hour came and went and still the redhead sat alone, nursing her drink. She spoke to no one and was quite obviously there all on her own. *Stupid bitch*, he thought. *Doesn't she read the papers?* Finally, without so much as a look to anyone, without making or receiving a phone call or text, she finished her drink, got up and straightened her skirt before she strolled past where James was sat and straight out the door. Smirking to himself, James downed the remainder of his drink and left the empty glass on the bar top as he too disappeared through the door and out into the night.

"Excuse me?"

She turned around, a startled expression on her face. "What do you want?"

"Sorry, I mean, um, er."

"Well?" she demanded, folding her arms defensively across her chest.

"Sorry, love, I saw you in the Acorn. You were on your own and well…"

"Jesus, what's the matter with you? Bit soft?" she asked sarcastically.

His eyes darkened. "No, I'm not soft. I saw you and thought I would, you know, try me luck and ask you out."

"Well, you're a bit late for that." She smiled at him, her mood relaxing. "I'm already out, aren't I?" she said teasingly.

"Yeah right. So do you fancy a drink with me then?"

"Well, I would love to, handsome, I really would," she said as her eyes rolled over his body. "But I gotta get the train, I'm afraid. I'm supposed to be meeting my friends in Bournemouth tonight; tell you what, give us your number so I can call you sometime."

James totally ignored her offer and his tone became aggressive.

"So what are you doing here then? Drinking all on your own?"

The woman was starting to feel slightly threatened by this man as she took a step back but tried to remain outwardly calm. Her defences were back up.

"Not that it's any of your business, but I thought I would have a quick one before getting the train."

"Have a drink with me, please."

"Sorry, but I really have to get on." She started to turn from him with every intention of getting away from him.

"I insist."

"I said no."

"Why? Think you're better than me, do you? Think you're too fucking good for me, do ya?" he growled.

"Look, I'm going now. I wi—"

James was on her in seconds, his fist flashed as he struck her in the side of her head. She went down hard. He looked down at her, licking his lips as he studied her, his anticipation growing. He could not wait to feel her life leave her as his hands encircled her throat. But that must wait, he could hear voices coming. Quickly, he picked her up, draping one of her arms around his neck whilst he held the hand by his neck and held her firmly around the waist as he half carried, half dragged her unconscious body towards his car.

"Hey, man, you okay there?"

Shit. He glanced over his shoulder to see a group of three young men looking at him. "Nah, you're okay, lads. Thanks anyway. Stupid bitch always does this to me, we go out and she always drinks way too fucking much. It's fucking embarrassing, ya know?"

"Yeah," one called back. "Well, good luck." They walked off, laughing to themselves and taking the piss out of James and his 'girlfriend'.

"Fucking morons," he muttered as he pressed the key fob in his pocket, unlocking the dark blue Vauxhall Vectra parked in front of him. Opening the door, he muscled the limp young woman into the passenger seat and very thoughtfully, put the seatbelt around her. There was no way James Pembleton would be caught by the pigs for something as stupid as not wearing a seatbelt.

Quickly going around to the other side, he climbed in and fastened his own seatbelt before starting the engine and driving out of the pub carpark. He turned the right indicator on and drove off, heading for his caravan home and the building site where the other seven from this area already lay buried beneath the rapidly growing new village of Castleleigh.

There was no security as such on the site. Unless you counted some geriatric, half blind, half deaf guy who walked around twice a night. *The old coot wouldn't see or hear anything if I offed her right in front of him*, James thought as he pulled up next to his caravan.

He got out of the car, leaving the unconscious woman inside; retrieving a set of keys from his jean pocket, James opened the door to his caravan and stepped up inside.

Several minutes later, James emerged carrying a small rucksack; he casually walked around the car and opened the passenger door. Kneeling down in the open doorway, he placed the rucksack in the footwell and took the woman's handbag from her arm. Unzipping it, he rummaged until he found what he was looking for—her driving licence.

"Hello, Karen," he whispered, looking from the licence and back to the woman.

"You and me are gonna be close friends, well, briefly anyway." He leant in, taking a handful of her red hair, letting it trail around and between his fingers. James sniffed it as you would a bunch of flowers.

"Aahh. Karen, you are divine, now let us get you out of those things."

He unzipped the rucksack and removed a large pair of scissors. Grasping her hair, he cut from close to the scalp; long red locks came away in his hand, which he tied in a knot, smelling it once more before tucking it in his pocket. He ripped greedily at her blouse; the buttons disappeared somewhere in the car as he pulled it off her.

James cut her bra between the cups and the shoulder straps, before pulling it away and letting her breasts fall loose. He was not interested in her nakedness; sex was not his goal. Fear was what James Pembleton relished, and before she died, Karen would be utterly terrified. He slipped the scissors' edge under the waistband of her skirt and cut the length until it came apart and then tugged and pulled it out from under her. He sliced twice through the waistband of her knickers, again pulling them from under her and lastly and carefully, he removed her sandal shoes.

James Pembleton stepped back to admire his handiwork, as he stared down at the unconscious and very vulnerable naked form of Karen Bennett.

"Now you are mine, you will wake soon. And when you do, hmmm, you will know the true meaning of terror. You will beg, you will offer and promise me anything and everything. And guess what? I will laugh at you whilst I kill you."

Gathering up her torn and cut clothing, he stuffed it all into the rucksack, taking the hair from his pocket and putting that in last. He zipped the bag up and walked back to his caravan. He opened the door and tossed the bag inside. Moving to the end of his caravan by the towing hitch, James took his old and rusty wheelbarrow by its handles and pushed it around to the still open passenger door of his car.

Taking hold of Karen under her arms, he dragged her from the car and dumped her unceremoniously into the wheelbarrow. He straightened her legs so they fell over the end without getting in his way whilst her head and neck lolled over the other end between the handles.

Whistling a tune to himself, James unravelled the hosepipe hanging on the fence next to his caravan. Once he had it, he aimed it at Karen's stomach and twisted the nozzle; the freezing cold spray hit her hard with its full force. He moved the angle, allowing the spray to hit her full in the face just as she came coughing and spluttering back to a confused and shocked state of consciousness. James turned the water off and smiled down at her terrified, disbelieving face.

"What? Who?"

"I thought you may want that drink now," James replied, laughing at his own joke.

She struggled to sit up, crying out as the rusty sides cut into her flesh as she tried. James put his large hands on her shoulders, forcibly pushing her back down, scraping her back in the process. She looked up into his eyes, her own huge and terrified, full of pained tears as she tried to make sense of what was happening to her.

"Who are you, please, please?" She cried, "Why are you doing this?" James silenced her as he struck Karen with a hard backhand across her cheek and nose. A sick grin crossed his lip as he saw the blood begin to flow from her nose.

"I got a special place all ready for you," he said, crouching down, his face millimetres from hers.

"We dug it this morning, it's due to be filled in Monday morning so it is perfect for our needs. You see, I dug it too deep so no one will find you once you're buried there and we concrete you in Monday morning."

The look on her face was fantastically beautiful to him, it went through many changes. From confused, to uncertainty, to disbelief. Her terrifying predicament slowly dawned on her face with shock and fear and finally terror. Karen had no words, her voice lost to her as she tried to understand and grasp hold of her churning emotions.

The whole time, James continued to smile that freaky evil smile down at her as he enjoyed the moment. She lay still in the wheelbarrow, paralysed with fear, her body unable and unwilling to follow the command of her brain to jump up and run. She was at his mercy and totally unable to fight him.

"Right then, shall we be off?" James said merrily as he picked up the handles, tilting the wheelbarrow and starting off at a brisk pace across the building site, Karen lying helpless within and frozen with both the cold and fear. The wheelbarrow bounced along over the uneven ground as James aimed towards a foundation pit at the rear of the site. The hole was big, nearly fifty feet by thirty, and almost six feet deep except for the end where James stopped the wheelbarrow; that was freshly dug and nearly ten foot deep.

If she wasn't so paralysed with fear, Karen would have seen the huge mound of dirt piled up next to her one-wheeled chariot at the edge of the pit. As James came to a stop, he just let go of the handles, letting the wheelbarrow bang down hard and causing Karen to nearly fall out.

The sudden shock was enough though to bring her back to reality. She thrashed and struggled in her attempt to get out and succeeded only by tipping it over and half falling, half rolling out onto the uneven and cold wet ground. James grinned as he looked on at Karen, as she struggled, with amused interest. He saw all of the various cuts and scratches she had received from the old rusty wheelbarrow, clearly visible on her milky pale skin.

How pleased James was that Karen had seemed to lose her voice completely; there was no whining to listen to, no asking of stupid questions and no need for him to talk to her, yet. That would come, as would the begging and the pleading just before he would end her worthless life. Oh, there were looks, of course, looks of accusations, looks of confusion and his most favourite look: the look of absolute and complete helpless terror.

The weather picked that exact moment to unleash itself upon them; it rained, and hard. Stinging drops of rain poured down on them. James loved that. It would, he knew, give him more enjoyment as he snuffed out her life.

Karen felt as if she were being stabbed by thousands of tiny needles, over and over. The cold hard rain beat down upon her naked body, stinging painfully with each and every touch.

Advancing upon Karen as she crouched in the slippery mud, James smiled at her, a grin of pure evil as he contemplated her fate. He grabbed her by the wrists, pulling her to her feet as he continued to stare into her eyes. She stood stock still in front of him as he ran his huge calloused hand up her arms to her shoulders and up to her neck. His fingers separating and stretching as he reached her slender neck, his thumbs almost joined at her throat.

"A little taste, my sweet," he whispered in her ear, his low voice barely audible over the hammering of the rain, and he squeezed. He could feel the muscles in her neck tighten against his hands as Karen gasped, struggling for breath, the moving of her lower jaw against his fingers as she tried to open her mouth to draw breath. The hands came next as her eyes bulged wide in terror. Karen grabbed hold of James's hands, clawing and pulling in a vain attempt to free herself.

James finally released his hold on her. Karen collapsed to her hands and knees at his feet, gasping for breath as her head hung below her shaking shoulders. The rain continued to pound down on Karen, her hair hanging in front of and hiding her face. The mud was splattering back up at her wrists and thighs with the force of the impacting rain whilst slowly her hands and knees sank into the sloppy ground. An intense pain hit her right side as she found herself lifted off the ground only to land on her back in a cold and deep muddy puddle. As she laid there, the rain hammering her body and face she realised that the pain was the giant kicking her.

She tried to look up at him but could not open her eyes against the rain, but she could feel the heavy pressures on her stomach and hips as James sat himself down on her.

"Did you like that, Red?" he asked gently. "No, I don't suppose you did, but it felt wonderful to me as your pulse quickened under my touch."

He leant in closer, his elbow digging in her chest painfully; a small whimper of pain escaped her lips as he did. James stroked the wet red hair from her face, running his fingers through it and curling it around his fingers.

He pulled, hard.

Karen's eyes flew open with the fresh pain and hate as she stared into the face of the monster clutching her hair in his massive hand. Tears, invisible against her rain-soaked face, chased the raindrops down her cheeks. Her mouth was open in a pained grimace, she tried to force out words, questions, a desperate plea. It was no good, she could say nothing, and all she could do was stare.

All of a sudden, the pain in her scalp from the pulling hair was gone, as was the weight upon her. He was grabbing at her shoulders and arms then, his fingers digging in painfully as he turned her. Karen twisted her neck as she was forced down into the mud; he was on her shoulders, his knee pressing her hard. Karen's mouth was shut tight as half of her mouth, nose and one eye became submerged in the freezing cold mud.

"No no no," James hissed at her. "This will not do, my dear." Grabbing her head with both hands, he twisted it back straight so her whole face became submerged in the freezing thick gloop that was forcing itself into her nose and ears.

She dared not breathe, she dared not struggle as that would only lead to more pressure upon her head. Something scratched her eye, digging at it, stabbing. Her head was forced deeper and the flint pushed against her eyelid, building a sharp pressure against her eyeball. She could hear muffled laughter through the rain; he was enjoying this and the bastard was laughing at her.

Karen thought that the flint would pierce her eyelid and stab straight through her eye; she knew it was coming right up until her back exploded with pain. She instantly drew a deep and agonised breath that filled her mouth and throat with mud and water. The pressure on her head was gone. Karen spat and coughed out the water as she lifted her head from the ground and curled up on her side, her body racked with coughs and splutters.

James loved it, he laughed with joy as he forced her head back down, further under. He didn't want to kill her yet, just terrify and hurt her. He let go of her head, so far gone she was that Karen did not try to move her head. James stood up and stamped, hard on her lower back, just above her backside. That got a response, her head flew back, brown water spilling from her lips as she curled onto her side, crying and coughing.

James sat down beside her, half lifting her body and cradling her head almost lovingly in his lap. "There, there. Come on, Red, it's okay now. Come, eat this."

Digging a huge handful of sloppy mud up in his hand, James pulled her head back once more as he hit her full in the face. The mud was forced over her lips as he packed it in, he pushed more up her nose, blocking it and so forcing her mouth to open once more in a desperate but vain attempt to draw breath into her body.

With Karen's mouth open again, he packed more and more into her until it spilt and dribbled back over her lips. With the palm of his hand, James forced her eyelid open; with his other hand, he rubbed the scratchy wet mud against her naked eyeball. Karen just lay in his arms taking the punishment. James was sorely disappointed; she had given up.

"You stupid fucking weak bitch, come on and fight, I ain't done with you yet," he screamed at her unmoving form.

With all of his enormous strength, James punched Karen as hard as he could in her stomach. Mud literally exploded from her mouth and nose as the air in her body was forced up and out of her. Karen just lay still across his lap; her muddy face slowly being washed clean by the still pounding rain. Karen was still breathing, James watched as her chest rose and fell. But he was so disappointed with her complete lack of any struggle.

"Pathetic, you ain't put up no fight. I like it when you bitches fight back. Aahh, Karen, but you should have seen Abigail last week. But she was a feisty one, a real fighter; she clung to her miserable life like no other. What a woman, I tell you, she nearly got away as well. But I had to put her down and hard. She's buried over there, by the way," he pointed but Karen still lay there, unmoving.

"Over by the new build there, she's in the foundation now and she ain't the only one, see. I got seven of you bitches buried here, and this ain't the first site I worked. I been doing this for years now, my tally stands at thirty-one women; you will make number thirty-two. Had to do a few blokes over the years too, oh yeah, some got nosey and some were boyfriends. They're the worst, fucking interfering boyfriends and husbands. Still, their faces are sheer art when they finally realise that the guy stood in front of them did their missus. Done me about eleven blokes now, everyone detailed in me book. All me birds and blokes, I like to collect paper clippings and stuff that I like to read sometimes. It gives me a real pleasure to relive what I like; a scrapbook…yoaaaaarrrgggghhh…"

James screamed as Karen gripped his balls in her hand and squeezed, pulling at them with all of her strength. As she sat up fast, letting go, her other hand smashed up into his nose, palm first. Had she been in a better state of mind,

Karen would have appreciated the feel of shattering nose cartilage beneath her hand. But not now, she had to get away.

She rose to her knees and slowly to shaky, unsteady feet. Water and mud cascaded down her as it poured from her body. Karen looked down at the writhing form of James Pembleton as he struggled to control himself and rise.

A burning and unbelievably bright light suddenly blinded Karen as it hit her full in the face. "What the hell is going on here?"

The security guard, Karen thought.

"Help me, please," Karen croaked at the old man as he stood still, pointing his torch at her.

James rose to his feet and covered the distance between himself and the guard in less than a second, he had the guard's craggy neck in his hands and squeezed. He could feel the old man's brittle bones disintegrate beneath his powerful fingers.

The old man was dead before he even knew James had him. James let go and the guard fell in a heap at his feet, dead. "That's twelve," he snarled. "Now then, bitch. It's your fucking turn," he growled, turning to face Karen.

James Pembleton turned around just in time for his face to meet the spade Karen was swinging at him. It hit him square in the face, smashing his already ruined nose and splitting his lips wide open. Karen held the spade tightly as she stared at the bloody ruined face of the man who wanted to kill her.

"You like a fight, do you?" he spat at her through ruined lips.

She swung again; the spade's edge caught him above the eye. With the downward momentum of the swing, the spade gouged a deep trench through his eye and across half his face. James howled in agony.

"Is this good enough for you?" Karen screamed as she hit him with all her strength in his kneecap. With his kneecap shattered, James could not support himself and collapsed face down in a heap.

"Get up, you bastard, I ain't finished with you yet." He did not move.

Dropping the spade, Karen knelt in the mud and leaning over his prone form, she used all her strength to turn James over onto his back. Karen forced herself to carry on against objections from her badly beaten body that screamed out at her in protest; she straddled him across his chest. Her hands made small fists that hit him over and over. She beat at his chest and his shattered face. Finally, exhausted and unable to hit out again, she stopped. Karen knew that she was spent and couldn't go on, but she also knew she had to finish it. If she didn't, Karen knew she was as good as dead.

"Was this good for you, you sick fuck?"

Her small hands struggled to encircle his muscular throat but she managed, she could feel as his fast pulse beat fiercely beneath her hands as she squeezed with all of the strength remaining in her.

"You need to try harder than that, you fucking bitch."

His hands shot up between her arms, knocking them easily aside, he had her firmly by the throat. Karen could no longer fight him, and she stopped as her arms fell limply away and her hands landed in the soft, cold and wet mud beside him. Karen would have collapsed too if not for James Pembleton holding her upright by her throat.

James snarled, his torn lips pulling back from his bloody gums as he strangled the life from the bitch that had hurt him so bad, but he loved the pain. He loved all pain; he loved to issue pain so he really couldn't complain about his own. He relished it, used it to make him stronger. He used his own pain to inflict more pain and damage upon this stupid woman. He watched the pain in her eyes, he saw them begin to glaze over and he could see the life leaving her.

James felt himself letting her go; his hands slipped away from her throat and found his own. He brought his hands up to his eyes, the rain washing the blood covering them away quickly. Confused, he stared up at Karen; he stared at the gushing blood fountain pulsing against her stomach. He looked at her utterly exhausted and battered but strangely triumphant face. He looked at her arm and his gaze slowly fell to her hand and the sharp jagged flint that it held.

You killed me, you fuckin killed me, was the last conscious thought to ever cross the living mind of the mass murderer known as James Pembleton.

It took Karen a long time to be able to move, let alone get up and seek help. After an age, she fell from the body and crawled on hands and knees back to the caravan where she retrieved her handbag and more importantly, her mobile phone. She called the emergency services, but passed out before she could describe her location properly.

Not being many huge building sites in Dorchester, the police found her quickly. She was admitted to hospital suffering not only from her ordeal but the freezing cold conditions her naked body had been exposed to for so long. Apart from a permanent blur in her left eye, Karen made pretty much a full recovery in time, at least physically.

The police made a thorough search of all property belonging to James Pembleton, his car and caravan where he lived. They found a large scrapbook that detailed the murder of forty-two people. The details contained within were staggering. James had written the exact circumstances, methods used and burial places. The book was complete with various newspaper clippings. With the details of each and every victim was several photographs taken before and after their murders. Names, dates and places where neatly written on the reverse.

There was no room in the ensuing investigation for doubt; every murder was premeditated, well planned and executed with a cold efficiency. It would be several years however until all of his victims would be found and finally laid to rest in a true grave by caring friends and family.

The good news was undisputed. One of England's deadliest and most terrifying serial killers of all time was dead and could consequently never hurt another living soul again.

Chapter 9
2012 – Haunted Hunters

Tom clapped his friend on the shoulder as they walked confidently towards the house. "Come on, buddy, let's go find us some spooks."

Tom opened the front door whilst Andrew twisted his torch on and moved slowly past him. He shone it forward, illuminating the hallway before them. Tom closed the front door behind them and looked where Andrew was pointing the beam of light. "You wanna go that way?" he asked, his voice hushed as he watched the light disappear into the gloom of the sitting room.

"Might as well, man, we're down here. Make sense to start here, don't you think?"

"Okay, lead the way. Oh Andy, just one thing?"

"What?"

"Why the hell are we whispering?" Tom asked, grinning.

Andrew laughed quietly as he turned back. "I don't know. It just seems like the right thing to do," he said in as close to his normal voice as he could muster, whilst smirking.

"Okay," Tom said, "time to get serious." He pulled the digital recorder from his jacket pocket whilst Andrew turned off his torch and powered up the hand-held night vision camera. Tom checked that the static camera and voice recorder was on and recording. He could not have explained why, but Tom was starting to get a slightly unnerving feeling, something was off but he couldn't quite put his finger on it. Determined though, he pushed the thought to one side and started.

"Okay, this is Tom and Andrew, EVP session number one in the sitting room." He took a deep breath. "Is there anyone here in this place with us?" He waited. "Can you hear me?" Tom glanced around in the gloom; the only light came from Andrew's camera.

"We aren't here to hurt you; we only want to help you. The Phillips family asked us to come, they are scared of you. We aren't, my name is Tom. This other man with me is Andrew."

"Hello." From Andrew.

"We mean you no harm, can you try and communicate with us?" Tom waited, hoping for a reply of some kind. "If you can, please try touching one of us. Or move something, tap or bang on something or touch one of us."

Tom did not worry that he had repeated himself. He was still new at this and was desperate to catch some activity; besides, being repetitive may have yielded results. Tom turned in a complete circle as Andrew followed him with the camera.

Both men stopped and stood still in the darkness, listening out for any noises, any movements. They did not move for a minute or so. There was no noise save for the ticking of a clock and the everyday background noises of a house, such as the freezer humming away to itself in the kitchen.

It was Andrew that finally broke the silence. "Man, this ain't happening," he said, frustration clear in his voice. "Are you here or not? Can you do anything or is the family that lives here lying and making you up?"

Tom frowned in Andrew's direction, slightly annoyed. "Really, Andrew, is that what you really think? Do you honestly believe I would be here if I thought that the paranormal was all rubbish?" Tom didn't like arguing, but Andrew's attitude had really gotten his back up.

"Sorry, Tom, look, I really am. But you hear so much bullshit all the time about this sort of thing. Hell, god knows I have to hear it from Jess all the damn time. I mean, all the crap she reads or watches. She believes anything she's told."

Tom stood in front of his friend. "Listen mate, no one forced you into this, but this is for real, okay. Sarah really thinks that something is definitely going on here. Look, I know we can't agree completely on this stuff and probably never will, but let's just try and do the best job we can. Like I said, Sarah believes."

"And you, Tom, what do you think?"

Tom paused for a moment before answering, "I wouldn't be here if I didn't believe in Sarah. Now I will admit that there doesn't seem to be anything in here with us at the moment, but you never know. Hell, I'm no expert on the spirit world, that's Paul's department, but I have this feeling. And if we're not successful, then maybe the girls will have more luck. Come on, let's try upstairs. EVP session ended." Tom pressed the pause button, walked out the door and headed for the staircase. He was angry with himself for not thinking to pause the machine earlier; their conversation had just been recorded. Everyone would now be able to listen to their disagreement.

Andrew followed, the light from his camera enabling Tom to see where he put his feet. When they reached the upstairs landing, Tom headed straight for the bathroom.

"Hey, Andy," Tom tried to make his tone light, hoping that they were over their argument and could move on as friends again. "Can you film the bath for me?"

"Yeah sure, just remind me not to come over to your place for a movie night," Andrew said, he was obviously thinking and trying to do the same thing.

Tom shook his head smiling as he turned the bath's hot tap on, his anger at Andrew now past and forgotten. He put his hand under the fast-flowing stream of water then held it up to the light from the camera. "No blood. Guess I shouldn't really be surprised. I mean, it's not like we're in some cheesy horror movie or anything. Andy, get a close up of the water, we need to document everything. Film it so there is no argument as to what was in the taps. This way, you, and everyone else who watches this tape, can see it's only clear plain water and not blood."

Andrew did as he was asked, then turned to Tom. "Listen, man, I'm not trying to be funny, but not to piss on your fireworks or nothing, that's two for two."

"Only for us, and it is still early. And from what the family told us, I still say the girls will be the ones to get a response from whatever is here. Don't worry, mate, we have a plan to try and lure things out."

"Uh oh, I don't know if I like the sound of that. What idiotic scheme have you got planned?"

"Don't worry, it's not much. I know Sarah and Jess have been talking and coming up with ways to encourage anything here to come forward for them."

"Riiight." Tom could tell Andrew wasn't convinced by the way he exaggerated the word. He didn't want to start another argument, but Tom knew Andrew wasn't going to like what he heard. Tom took a deep breath.

"The girls have got a plan, it's nothing really. Sarah said she was just gonna take a quick bath, while er, you know, Jessica goes and takes a lie down in the daughter's bed."

Tom didn't have to wait long for Andrew's outburst. The atmosphere changed in an instant. You could have cut it with a knife as Andrew yanked the light cord, flooding the bathroom in a blinding fluorescent light. He looked Tom dead in the eyes, his voice emotionless.

"Listen to me, Tom, we're friends, okay. I respect you and I love Sarah like a sister, and Jess is my sister. You know me, you know I don't believe in this stuff and to be totally honest with you, I think it's complete bollocks. But if there is the slightest chance," he held his thumb and finger close as he leaned towards Tom. "The slightest chance of anything going on in this damn place, then my sister is no way going to be left anywhere on her own."

Andrew shook his head. "And if you want to leave your missus naked and alone in a bathtub where some other bird supposedly already got herself strangled. Not to mention that bloody asshole Paul prowling about; man, you're a bigger fucking idiot than I thought." Andrew turned and stormed out, leaving Tom alone to his thoughts.

Tom pulled the light cord, instant darkness descended upon him, leaving him effectively blind. Tom wanted to go charging after Andrew, he wanted to explain and try to make things right. But instead, he just stood still in the dark silence.

They're mine.

"What the hell!" Tom shot out into the hallway. "Andy," he called. "Andrew, was that you?" Tom heard the angry footfall as Andrew came out of Susan and Brandon's bedroom.

"Was what me?" he snapped.

"That voice, did you say something just then?"

"No, I didn't say anything." He sighed, trying to calm his tone. "Sorry, I didn't mean to snap. I thought I would leave you alone for a few minutes while I let off some steam on my own and calmed down."

"That's okay mate, listen. I don't know if it's this house or what, we're both a bit highly strung at the moment. And to be fair, you're probably right about the girls. I will talk to Sarah about it when we get out. But just then when I called you. I swear, I just heard a bloody voice."

"What did it say?"

"I'm not sure, it sounded like 'mine' or something like that. I didn't really hear properly what it said, only that it said something," Tom said, his voice cracking slightly with apprehension.

"Okay, calm down, man. Calm down. Now this [was a] woman talking?"

"Shit man, I don't know." Tom smacked the wa[ll, "I'm] not even sure anymore. It could have been cos I [was] hearing things." Tom shrugged and walked aw[ay from the] bedroom Andrew had just been in. Andrew stayed [there,] listening, hoping to hear any further voices for himself.

"Come on then, say something to me," Andrew challenge[d.] "What, you liked it when we argued, did you? Are you making us argue[? Where] did that come from? "Or was it the talk about the girls that you liked?" Andrew heard nothing but the bed springs creaking where Tom had sat down on the bed in the parents' room. Realising that he was wasting his time as he wasn't getting any luck where he was, Andrew decided to join Tom in the bedroom.

Andrew stopped dead in his tracks at the doorway and stared uncertainly through the gloom at where Tom stood across the far side of the room, next to the dressing table with the large mirror on it.

Hearing his friend enter the room, Tom turned around. "What?" he said, a little harsher than he intended to.

"How long have you been stood there?" Andrew asked.

"I don't know, one minute, two minutes maybe, since I came in, why?"

"Did you sit on the bed?"

"For Christ's sake, Andy, no. I just said I've been over here, now why the hell would I have sat on the bed, only to get straight back up again?"

"Listen, Tom, please. I'm trying here, I really am, okay? I was outside trying to hear your 'voice', I didn't hear anything out there, so when I heard the bedsprings creaking in here, I thought I would come in with you so we can try and carry on with the investigation."

"And?"

"And? Jesus, Tom, just think about it for a second. I heard the bedsprings creak and came in. You're on the other side of the bloody room and say you never even sat on the bed. Are you sure you didn't lean on it as you walked past or something?"

"Positive, but that's great," Tom said excitedly. "That's twice we've heard something now."

"It's something, I'll admit that, but it's nothing conclusive, Tom. You heard something out on the landing where there are no recorders. From the same place,

ng in here, which you didn't. I admit that if I was a believer, it
 ...nething, but come on, it hardly qualifies as a nine o'clock news
...does it?"

"...u're right, I'm sorry. I really don't mean to be such an arse. I guess this
...is just getting to me."

"It's cool, man, listen, I don't feel too comfortable here myself. And you
...ever know your luck, maybe the recorder in here picked it up. We can find out when we review it later. Come on, let's go check the girl's room, then get out of here. Let the girls walk around because at the moment, I'm still very far from convinced."

"But you heard the bed."

"I thought I did, Tom, but houses make noises. There is no solid proof yet, come on, let's go."

Tom followed Andrew to Alice's bedroom, he tried not to feel too disappointed but deep down, he knew Andrew was right. The 'voice' he had heard could have been from any number of things. He hadn't actually heard the words clearly so he had no choice but to discard it. And as for the bed noise, Andrew was right; that too could have been anything. Many times, as he lay in bed with Sarah, listening to her breathing as he tried to get to sleep. The noises their house made when all was quiet…well, it was amazing they ever got to sleep.

He sat down on the bed and watched Andrew walk around the room, filming everything with his camera. Andrew turned to face him. "You want to do any EVP or call it a day?"

Tom was not ready to give up and let Andrew have it all his own way, yet. "We're here to do a job, so let's get to it and find proof." He paused. "One way or another."

Tom stood and pressed the record button on his digital recorder. "Okay, this is Tom and Andrew, EVP session number two in Alice's bedroom."

Tom called out, "Hello, is there anybody here with us?" He paused, listening. "Please, you do not have to be afraid of us. We are not here to hurt you. We only want to talk to you. And see you, if you are willing and able to let us."

"Do you like it here?" Silence followed Tom's question.

"Did you die in this area?" Tom continued as Andrew scanned around with the camera.

"Are you happy here? Do you need help?" Tom looked up at Andrew, who shook his head in reply.

"Can you make a noise or touch one of us?" Andrew moved to the girl's chest of drawers and tapped the top with his knuckles. "Like this, can you do it?" He tapped again; still nothing.

"Do you not want us here? Do you want us to go? If you do, you're going to have to do something." Tom paused his questioning for a moment. "If you want us to go then you will have to make your presence known and tell us."

"Hey, Tom?" Andrew said quietly.

"Yeah."

"Get aggro with it, try and provoke it or something. Maybe it liked us arguing earlier," he said, moving the camera and focussing it on Tom.

Why not? Tom thought, shrugging. "You coward," Tom said. "You show yourself to and attack women, but you ain't got the nerve when it's two guys here, do you? What's the matter? Are you that weak that you can only have a go at women and young girls? You're pathetic, you offend me." More silence followed. "Shit," Tom said, holding his arms. "Andy, is it me or does it seem to have gotten colder in here to you?"

"Feels fine to me," Andrew replied. "Just the same as before. Why, you got something?"

"Must be my imagination but it sure feels colder, come over here." Tom took a step back as Andrew walked over, his hand out in front of him touching the air where Tom had stood.

"Feels a bit cooler I suppose."

"What do you think, could it be something?" Tom asked hopefully.

"Sorry, mate, I know it's not what you probably want to hear, but if I'm honest with you, this ain't nowhere near enough to convince me. Look, let's be honest for a sec. I'm the one you need to convince, I'm the sceptic, remember. Make a believer out of me, mate, and I will convince the world. But there has to be a million and one explanations for the temperature change, you know? Just say the word and I'll start hitting you with them."

Tom smiled. He couldn't help himself despite the disappointment he was feeling. "Yeah, I know, and yet again you're right," Tom said, almost a sigh. "EVP session finished."

He turned the recorder off and put it in his pocket as Andrew stopped filming. "Come on, Andy, let's get out of here."

They left the room together and trudged down the stairs. Tom couldn't help but feel disappointed and annoyed. He was so sure that they would have been able to capture something.

Tom opened the front door and together, they walked across the lawn to the car where the girls and Paul waited for them. The front door of the car opened and Sarah jumped out. "How did it go, guys? We saw you through the cameras, you looked a bit excited a couple of times. Did you find anything?"

Andrew shook his head and smiled at Sarah. "Nope, not a thing. Like I said, there is no such thing as ghosts."

Tom was slightly more forthcoming and told them everything that had happened, including the possible voice and creaking bed. "Obviously, nothing conclusive, but a couple of personal experiences was still something. And the fact that Andy heard something as well—"

"Yeah, but, Tom, like we said, those creaks could have come from anywhere," Andrew interrupted, desperate to hold on to his non-believer status.

"My brother, the eternal sceptic," Jessica said, hugging Andrew's arm. "Guess it's up to us girls then. Sarah, you ready?"

"Yeah, but before we go…Paul." Paul came wandering over and looked up as Sarah called his name.

"Paul, can you shed any light on any of this for us?" Sarah asked; more to try and make Paul feel a part of the group than to actually want to talk to him. His reply left her wishing that she hadn't bothered.

"I'm not a miracle worker, you know. Had I actually been allowed to enter the property, I may have heard the voice and been able to tell you who it was and what it said. However, as good as I am, it really isn't easy to translate something that wasn't heard and may or may not be a figment of imagination. As for the squeaky bed, well what can I say about that? No, I'm sorry; I have never communicated with the other side through bed springs." Sarcasm was never far from Paul's lips, neither did he lack in the ability to sulk. "Perhaps I should go and wait in the car whilst you girls go in without me and work your wonderful magic. I will wait for when you come back. Maybe then I can use my skills to explain how to communicate through hairdryers."

"Tom, please try and keep mister helpful here happy, will you?" Tom nodded, trying not to laugh at Paul's tantrum. "Jess, you got the bag?"

"Yep."

"Hey, Sarah, hang on. Have you got a sec before you go in?" Tom asked whilst looking across at Andrew.

"Yeah sure, hun, what's up?" Sarah asked as Tom put his arm across her shoulders and guided her several feet away from the others, well out of earshot. Tom turned to face her, searching her eyes.

"Listen, love, me and Andy were talking, and we're both a little worried about you two. Are you sure about this?"

The confused look Sarah gave him made Tom explain himself further. "This whole lone vigil thing, you know, the bath thing I mean. You do know that you're gonna be all on your own in there? Jess will be off in another room and we'll be out here." Tom's voice trailed off as he hung his head slightly. "I don't know, if anything happens to you…" He left the statement unfinished.

Sarah took Tom's head in her hands and lifted it so she could see his eyes. "Trust me, Tom, nothing will happen. Jess and I will only be separated by the hallway, one room away from each other. And besides, I only plan to half fill the tub. I promise you, nothing will happen." Sarah leant in and kissed Tom tenderly on his lips, before grinning like the Cheshire cat and pulling away from him.

"What?" Tom couldn't help but smile back, he always found her smile infectious.

"It's really sweet and everything, but I'm really more worried about you." The blank look Tom gave her made Sarah smile all the more. "You're the one who has to put up with Paul." She turned to walk away, Tom caught her arm and pulled Sarah back into a hug.

"Just promise me," he asked anxiously. "Anything slightly off happens in there, and you two get out. No messing, no stalling, you get out. Promise me."

Sarah hugged him tightly, she whispered in his ear, "I, we will. I promise you."

"Come on then, let's get you in there."

Walking back to the group hand in hand, Sarah winked at Jessica. She let go of Tom and crossed to Andrew; she gave him a quick hug. "We'll be fine, don't worry. See you soon." Andrew smiled, nodding his understanding at her. Sarah turned to Jessica.

"Okay, let's do it. See you guys soon."

Sarah and Jessica, the latter with a camera in hand and rucksack on her shoulder, set off across the lawn and disappeared through the front door.

With Sarah in the lead, torch in hand, the girls made their way down the hallway and into the sitting room just as the guys had previously. Jessica wasted no time; as soon as they entered the sitting room, she had the camera on and began panning the room. Sarah got out and switched on her digital recorder.

"Ready, Jess? Here we go. Sarah and Jessica, EVP in the sitting room." Sarah took a deep breath. "Is there anyone here?"

Jessica continued scanning the room with the camera as they waited, hoping for a response. Unfortunately, as with the guys, no response was forthcoming. Sarah called out some more but still no noises or voices were heard.

"Hey, Sarah, shame this isn't one of those television shows, we would have had all sorts of bangs and footsteps from all over the place by now." She smirked. "Hell, one of the guys would have probably gotten angry or fainted as well."

Sarah laughed, but couldn't help but think that Andrew and Tom had come out looking far from happy with each other. "And I thought you were a huge fan of all those shows?"

"I am, but that doesn't stop you from realising when they're faking stuff. Still, having said that, I did find a good show recently. Hell, even Andy sits still and watches it with me."

Sarah almost choked on her laugh. "There goes his reputation, it must be goo—"

Sarah looked up at the ceiling above them at the exact same second Jessica looked up with the camera. "Did you hear that?"

Jessica managed a nod. "I, I think it came from upstairs."

"It did, I swear that was a couple of footsteps."

"Maybe I shouldn't have mentioned those shows. What do you want to do?"

Sarah was nervous, she was, if totally honest, a little frightened. But she had a job to do and she intended to get it done. "I say we go up, it's what we're here for, after all. Let's try and find where it's coming from. What's above us?" Sarah asked, more to herself as she thought. Jessica shrugged. Sarah continued, "I think it's the main bedroom, Susan's room. Jess, you lead the way, I'm right behind you."

Slowly, Jessica made her way to and up the stairs. Sarah was on her heels, squinting through the darkness in an attempt to see anything. They got to the top of the stairs and made their way into the main bedroom. Jessica scanned around with the camera in the hope of catching something. Sarah tried calling out a few more times but there were no further noises to be heard.

"My bloody heart is doing ten to the dozen," Jessica whispered. "I can't believe we heard that. What now?"

Sarah thought about it for a moment or two, she considered the options then said, "Do you still feel up for doing a solo vigil?"

"Hell yeah, it's not like it's really all that scary, is it," she replied almost disappointedly. "I mean, it's great we heard those footsteps and all, but we need a lot more."

Sarah could say nothing about her own apprehension in front of Jessica, especially after what Jessica had just said. She would have felt more than just a little foolish, especially as the whole thing was her idea to start with. "Okay then, go get yourself off to bed then. I'm gonna take a bath. Let's see what happens," Sarah said, trying her hardest to make her voice sound confident.

They exchanged hugs and Jessica whispered in Sarah's ear, "Stay safe, babe, if you need me, I will only be across the landing, okay?"

"Don't worry, Jess, if anything actually happens and I need help, I expect the guys outside will hear my screams. But you take care as well, yeah? If you need anything, just shout."

"I will."

Sarah watched as Jessica left, leaving her alone in the dark. She looked all around. As the darkness settled down upon her, Sarah couldn't shake a feeling of being watched. She hastily made her way across the landing and into the bathroom. Sarah made sure she left the bathroom door slightly ajar as she took several deep calming breaths. Sarah looked around the white sterile room; the only light was from the street lights outside, casting everything a deathly grey colour. Sarah's whole body was covered in goose bumps as she slowly began to undress.

Jessica pushed the door open and entered Alice's bedroom; she smiled at the posters on the wall and thought how this could easily have been her room a few years ago. She crossed to the bed and pulled the covers off. Kicking off her trainers, Jessica climbed into the bed and pulled the covers back over herself. She lifted her arms from the duvet so she could point the camera around the room. Taking a few deep breaths, Jessica realised that this was real and the very first time that she would attempt this on her own. There was no one else with her, no help and she was actually going to try and talk to a spirit on her own. She called out.

"Hello? Are you here in this room?" Jessica panned the camera around, peering through the view finder. She saw and heard nothing until the sound came from within the wall behind her. Jessica jumped; she sat up fast looking around, one hand on her beating chest, she breathed heavily as she used her other hand to shakily guide the camera around towards the noise. With her heart beating a fast rhythm against her chest and arms shaking, Jessica tried to calm herself and focus. She lowered the camera to the bed and smiled to herself. "Get a grip, girl." She realised that the sound she was hearing was nothing but high-pressured water rushing through the pipes as Sarah was filling the bath.

That's wrong, she thought to herself. *I filled the bath earlier for Andrew.* Jessica was just about to get up and check on Sarah when common sense hit her. *The water must be freezing by now, I suspect she's just putting hot water in.*

Realising that it was nothing of importance, Jessica continued with her own vigil. "Is there anyone here with me?"

Jessica waited a moment. She gently patted the bed beside her.

"Come and sit with me. Hold my hand. I promise I won't hurt you, I just want to talk to you."

Jessica continued to gaze through the viewfinder around the room. Everything was cast in an eerie green that night vision caused. She paused on the desk in the corner. Upon it sat Alice's open (but switched off) laptop, her iPod, various pens and pencils, and her ring-bound notebook.

Jessica continued panning the camera. She slowly took in the whole room, from the boy band posters to the dirty washing stacked in a heap on the floor. She saw the bookcase full of, no doubt, the usual teenage vampire or romance books. *Or probably a combination of both*, Jessica thought. She continued scanning the room.

"Please talk to me. You like to be with Alice, don't you?" Jessica asked. "Come to me, I invite you now to be with me. Alice is scared, I'm not. Please, I want to talk to you." Bang.

"What the fuck?"

Jessica wasn't so much scared as shocked. The sudden noise in the dark had startled her and made her jump. Jessica panned the camera around the room, trying to spot what had caused the banging noise. She was pretty sure the noise came from her left side, over near the desk. The desk came into focus, the same as before. The laptop, iPod, notebook, pens and pencils. Jessica began to scan towards the bookcase.

The laptop.

Jessica scanned back. The laptop sat exactly where it had before, the lid closed, waiting for its teenage owner to pick it up.

That's not right, Jessica thought to herself. *I'm sure it was open before.*

Jessica was convinced that the noise that she had just heard had been the lid of the laptop slam close. She couldn't swear one hundred percent though that it had indeed been open before, and realised that it could be something important to watch out for, come analysis time.

"Did you do that, did you just close the computer?"

Jessica sat in silence, listening. Her heart nearly blasted itself out of her chest as she heard the terrified scream coming from the bathroom.

Sarah.

Jessica was out of bed and on her feet in seconds. She ran from Alice's room and across the hallway to where the bathroom door stood closed before her.

"Sarah, Sarah, are you okay in there?" Jessica called anxiously.

No answer. Jessica turned the handle whilst calling out to Sarah. "I'm coming in okay." Only silence came from the other side. Jessica started to worry about her friend.

The handle turned but the door didn't budge. Jessica rattled the handle, pumping it up and down whilst leaning into the door in an attempt to open it. "What the hell? Sarah, can you hear me?"

She shouted, "Unlock the damn door, I can't get in."

Jessica heard the lock disengage; the door immediately swung inwards. She stepped through the door.

Sarah unbuttoned her blouse; she was nervous about what she was going to do. She had decided though, and Sarah was the kind of person that once her mind was set, nothing would stop her. Removing her blouse, Sarah folded it and placed it on the closed toilet seat. Sarah looked down at the empty tub, she thought for a moment that she remembered Andrew saying something about filling the bath earlier. Obviously, she was wrong, Sarah decided, as the evidence of the empty bathtub in front of her said otherwise.

She leaned over and turned the bath taps on. Water exploded from the taps, the pressure was fantastic, Sarah could hear the water rushing through the pipes on its way to the bath.

She tested the temperature regularly, letting the bath fill nearly halfway; she turned the taps off. The silence was immediate and deafening. Sarah froze, lost for a moment in the sudden silence. A single drop of water that fell from the tap to splash in the bath brought her back to the present. She ran her hand through the water and brought it up to her face. Even in the gloom, she could clearly see that it was indeed nothing more than water.

Sarah shook her head and smiled, she realised that she had been needlessly working herself up and took some slow deep breaths to try and relax. After a few seconds, Sarah had calmed down. She pulled the waist button on her jeans open and then popped all of the fly buttons open. Kicking her shoes off, Sarah pulled her jeans down and off. Folding them, they joined her blouse on the toilet. She stood beside the bath in nothing but her red swimsuit, the one Tom loved to see her in. Thinking of Tom made her smile. She was determined and would make him proud.

Sarah leant a hand down on the bath's edge as she stepped in, one leg first and then the other. She looked down in amusement as her legs disappeared to mid-calf. She eased herself down to a sitting position and relaxed. Unsure whether to call out or not, Sarah decided to emulate what Susan had told her. She lay back in the bath, forcing the water level to rise, it rose until the water filled her ears. She lay peacefully listening to the hollow, echoing sound of water lapping against the side of the bathtub.

Sarah heard what sounded to her like a dull thump. It was not, she knew, coming from the bathroom. So figuring it was probably Jessica, she ignored it. Sarah lay still and enjoyed the warm surrounding comfort of the bath.

Sarah only felt the hand on her chest as it applied sufficient pressure to hold her still. Her eyes flew open at the exact time that a second, huge, calloused hand found her face. Its palm was on her chin, the little finger and thumb on either side of her cheeks, three fingers against her forehead. The fingers squeezed and pain shot through Sarah's face and head. She opened her mouth to scream as her head was pushed down hard. Sarah's face went back and under the surface, her mouth filled with a thick coppery tasting substance.

The pressure was suddenly gone. It went as quick as it came. There was no hand either pushing on her chest or face as Sarah sat up quickly. Her head burst through the water surface. Sarah gripped at the handrail on the bath's edge whilst leaning over the other side of the bathtub, coughing and spitting as she tried to get the foul taste from her mouth.

When the coughing wracking her body subsided, Sarah climbed on shaky legs from the tub. She reached for the light cord; Sarah yanked on it. Calming slightly with the bright light on, she turned to face the mirror.

Sarah let out a scream, one of sheer terror, at the face that was looking back at her. She could hardly recognise her own face under all the blood. Sarah's hair was hung in congealing strings of red across her scarlet-streaked face. Sarah ran her fingers down her cheek, leaving pink streaks in the blood-soaked face that looked back horrified and wide eyed at her. She looked down at her fingers as they slowly dripped blood.

The rattling of the door before it burst open caused Sarah to turn around. She stood face to face with an out-of-breath Jessica who stood with her mouth open, seemingly lost for words, staring at her. *It must be all the blood*, she thought.

"Sarah, are you okay? Why did you lock the door?" Jessica finally managed to ask breathlessly.

"Lock the door? No, I left it open."

"What happened, I swear to you it was locked, I couldn't get in. Are you okay?"

"Okay? No, no, I'm not okay," Sarah said incredulously. "He was here, Jess. He just tried to drown me in the blood."

"Blood? What blood? Jesus Sarah, what happened?" Jessica stared openly at her friend. "Sarah, what on earth are you talking about, you're shaking, come here." She went to her friend, pulled Sarah into a trembling hug, not caring about getting wet herself.

Sarah tried to resist, she tried to pull away from Jessica, but the girl managed to hold on to Sarah's shoulders. "No, Jess, you don't want this on you."

"Want what?" Jessica asked, looking Sarah up and down at arm's length. She saw nothing but her friend, slightly pale and shaking with cold and fear as she stood in front of her.

Sarah looked down at her own body. She ran her hands over herself and stared at her own palms. "What the hell?" She was wet and covered in goose bumps but there was no blood to be seen anywhere. She looked into the bathtub at the gently lapping water waves. Sarah turned tentatively to the mirror, only to see her slightly haggard and confused face staring straight back.

Jessica waved into and covered the static camera with a flannel before she helped Sarah dry off. She left her alone only briefly to retrieve her trainers and the rucksack from outside the room. Sarah was still shaking whilst Jessica helped her get dressed. Sarah tried to explain as best she could what she had seen.

Sarah even began to doubt herself as the two of them tried to make sense of it all. What they struggled with the most though were the guys, who were sat outside watching them through the static cameras. Even without sound, they could see almost everything, so why had no one come in to help when Sarah was being forced under the water?

The two of them left and headed back out to the car to try and get answers from Tom and the others.

"Honestly, Sarah," Tom said. "For the hundredth time, we saw nothing. To be honest, we didn't see anything that concerned us or anything unusual at all. We saw Jess leave the parents' room and go off into Alice's room. We saw her in the bed, presumably calling out whilst she filmed the room. The only thing that was odd was when she jumped up and ran to the bathroom. Before that, we saw you go into the bathroom, get undressed then have a bath. You got out just before Jess came in to you."

"What about me screaming though, what about the hands on me?" Sarah asked desperately, almost accusingly.

"There was none of that, love, all that we saw was just what I told you."

Smirking, Paul walked over. "If I may?"

"Be my guest," Sarah replied. "Because I don't have a damn clue what just happened in there."

"I think it is, in fact, very simple to explain. I think you simply fell asleep in the bath and dreamt it." He put his hand up to ward off Sarah's protests. "Think about it if you will, my dear, you have taken on rather a lot. Not to mention all of the stress you're under and stories you have heard. I think you fell asleep exhausted and your mind took over."

"Okay," Jessica said. "Then I want you to explain to me how and why the bloody bathroom door was locked?"

"Well, that is certainly no mystery. The door was locked quite simply because we watched Sarah lock it."

"What? No, I didn't." Sarah looked to Tom and Andrew for support.

Andrew replied first, "Look, Sarah…god, this is hard." He sighed. "Paul's right. There, I said it. We did see you shut and lock the door. But I know you, if you say something happened, then I'm prepared to listen. Something more than we know has to be going on here. And I know for a fact that you're not a bullshitter. If you're up for it, I'll go back inside that place with you. We will find the answers to what is happening. You can make me a believer."

"Oh, for crying out loud, really? You're not seriously going to go along with this nonsense, are you?" Paul implored Tom. "This girl," he gestured towards Sarah, "is too young, inexperienced and naïve to understand the things that are happening here. Quite frankly, I am disgusted at the antics that have been allowed to go on so far. I will go in and sort things out for you."

Paul would have been okay if not for the disrespectful description of Tom's girlfriend in front of Tom. Tom took two fast steps towards Paul before Sarah realised what was about to happen and managed to position herself so that she stood between them. Sarah looked Tom in the eye, silently begging him not to punch Paul.

After several seconds, Tom closed his eyes and nodded to her. Sarah then turned to Paul. She may have prevented Paul from getting hurt, but she no longer feared speaking her mind to him as she had after their first meeting. She was not about to let him off the hook completely.

"Listen to me," she spoke very quietly to Paul. "You are here because of us. I don't give a shit what you think of the rest of us. But you will damn well learn that this is my team. You are here at my discretion, and I can replace you without losing any sleep. Now I suggest you go get in the car, shut the hell up and keep the fuck away from me until I call for you, okay?"

Paul looked as if he had just been slapped in the face, He clearly wanted to answer Sarah back, but instead, he wisely turned on his heel and stormed off to sit in the car on his own. Sarah turned to Andrew.

"You still want to come in with a crazy woman like me? You're on, come on, let's do it."

Andrew smiled at Sarah as he looked at Tom for the go-ahead. Tom nodded at his best friend.

"Look after my girl."

"I will, mate. I promise."

Sarah and Andrew headed back to the house.

Chapter 10
2012 – Paul

"Thank you so much, Paul, I really can't tell you how wonderful it was to speak to my Michael again. I've missed my son so much. But thanks to you, I've found peace and can finally let him go."

"You are most welcome, Mrs Waters. Remember, to you, my door and services are always open. Any and all who need my help are always most welcome."

Paul waved at the woman, smiling at her tear-stained face as he closed the front door of his house and leant against the inside of it. "Moronic idiots," Paul muttered to himself as he withdrew the thick wad of twenty-pound notes from his shirt pocket and fanned through them.

Paul Ackermann was first and foremost a con artist. He preyed on the vulnerable, taking them for every penny he could whilst giving them false hope. Paul was a clever and observant man who could almost see what others were thinking. To him, grieving people were like an open book. This helped no end when he conducted his psychic readings for them.

It was so easy for Paul, a man without conscience or a moral compass, to manipulate the grieving. He thought of every last one of them as 'weak-minded fools'. He could convince them all that their loved ones were in communication with him, and that they could actually speak to them again through him. Paul would get close to his clients. He would become their friend and so get to know them and how they thought. He would ask masked questions, leading questions, and then use his knowledge to tell his clients what they wanted to hear.

When they left Paul's home, they would leave happy in their misguided belief that they had just spoken to a loved one on the other side. Paul would play his part well. He would watch them go whilst smiling sincerely and sweetly, satisfied with the one hundred pounds that he had just fleeced them for.

Paul was not a complete fake. On the contrary, he was far from it. On many occasions, Paul had indeed spoken to what many would describe as a spirit or ghost of one who had passed. It was, however, draining for him, not to mention the hard work it required maintaining a link with the other side. Contact and communication was never easy, hence it was far easier and a damned sight more profitable for Paul to fake it. He had a gift, but why use it when he could make far more money by lying, something that came naturally to Paul.

He couldn't understand why he should drain himself both physically and mentally for others when he could profit from their grief at no cost to himself. Paul was a parasite who enjoyed, relished in fact, the emotional pain and misery of others.

Paul was, for the most part, a loner. He detested the company of others, especially the ignorant. That consisted of, in Paul's belief, almost everybody that he had ever met. He had endured years upon years of taunts and jeers from the ignorant. He had suffered threats and actual abuse where his special talents were concerned. Paul was completely unable to see or even perceive that it was his own attitude towards others, which had led to this behaviour aimed at him.

Paul deeply resented the spiritual mediums that had been a success and found fame through their talents. He couldn't see that the simple difference was that instead of pretending to care for the grieving, they actually did care. Paul hated that he, talented as he was, remained in the large, an unknown.

Paul entered his sitting room, a fairly small room. What little space there was, it was given mostly over to his readings. A table sat in the centre of the room, which took up much of the space the room offered. The table had a crystal ball resting upon it, something that Paul felt helped create an air of authenticity.

Paul picked up his laptop from the top of his bookcase as he made his way over to and sat down at the table. He opened the lid and switched it on. Drumming his fingers on the table, Paul waited impatiently for the machine to boot up. He had never been a patient man and absolutely hated to be kept waiting for or denied anything. Finally, the laptop came online.

Searching the internet for his one release, Paul opened and downloaded the latest issue of his favourite e-magazine, 'Real Life Haunting in Great Britain'. It was in that magazine that Paul had come across the advert from Haunted Hunters. It was also whilst sat alone reading that magazine that Paul had received the first contact, the contact that would change his life forever. *Paul, you are the one.*

The faint voice startled Paul briefly. "Who are you?" Paul asked. He looked around for the source of the disembodied voice, recognising it for what it was.

My name is James, and I need your help.

"What do you need?" Paul was unused to being contacted so was slightly taken aback. This was strange as usually in true communication, he was the instigator. Paul was very wary of his 'visitor', but ultimately decided to pursue and discover the purpose that the spirit had for contacting him.

With your help, I can cross over into your world again. I can carry on my work in the living world.

"What?" Paul was stunned. "You would seek to remove the veil? Who the hell are you?"

Paul, for all of his many faults, was not a stupid man. He knew of the metaphysical veil that existed to separate the worlds. In fact, he had studied for many years the belief of such a veil. He had searched for the powers that others had claimed could be taken from the veil, if one could find the way to move freely through it. The ultimate power, however, was believed to be endowed on the one who could destroy the veil and remove it totally. Paul's interest was, without a doubt, aroused.

I told you who I am, if not necessarily what I am. Now listen to me and I shall tell you how you may become a god amongst men. My friend, I need strength. In your world, I was strong, I was a predator and I fed often. Here, in this realm, I am relatively new and considered weak, but with your help, I can become a power once more.

We can sometimes gain strength and interact with your world; it is not an easy thing and it takes a toll on my strength. We can sometimes have influence over the weak-minded, even control them to a degree. I cannot, however, as you surely know, fully cross over into your realm. Yet. That is where you come in, my friend.

You will receive a sign. It will lead you to others who in turn you must bring before us. Together, we will destroy their lives and so give power to us so that we may grow strong again. With your help and our new power, we will literally tear down the veil, the force that holds us prisoners in this accursed afterlife and separates our worlds. When we are free, we will instil great powers upon you. None living will be able to stand in your way or dare mock you ever again.

And I, I will hunt and kill as I see fit. I will be way beyond the reach of death, and therefore unstoppable.

Will you join us, Paul?

A thin smile spread across Paul's lips. "What's the catch?" he asked.

Paul knew the theory very well. If the dead could find a way to kill the living, then they would become more powerful, thanks to the spirit essence of their victim. If this continued and the dead could gain enough power, then the veil would simply cease to be.

Many believed the veil was created by the one great power from the energies of all the living. With the dead rising up against the living, the veil would swiftly weaken and be destroyed. Paul also knew, the theory at least, that if a living soul should rise up against the one power to join forces with the dead against the living, then that person could grow all powerful. Two questions remained to Paul: why him? And why now?

Aaahh, okay, the voice answered. *It is true that a few so-called champions of the one stand between us and the destruction of the veil. But they are nothing. They are less than nothing to us. We have been told by the old one, the Splitting Man, he who knows their strongest champion from before. He has said that as we grow stronger, their power will fade and they will fall before us. We will meet soon. Look for the sign, Paul. We, William and I, shall contact you again. Soon. Farewell.*

Thoughts of glorious power and the ultimate control of all others flashed through Paul's mind. He would have it all. He would be a master, a king, a god. A god amongst the lower mortals, he would make all the non-believers pay. His will be done.

Paul shook his head, clearing away the cloudy feeling that always remained after contact. He looked down at the screen on his laptop. The advert stood out clearly to him. Paul read it.

```
Have you had experience with the other side?
        Can you help us?
```

HAUNTED HUNTERS

We are a new paranormal investigation team and we are looking for a psychic medium to join us.
We seek to prove the existence of the afterlife to the world.
Can you help us?
If you can then please contact Sarah Jackson today
hauntedhuntersinvestigations@gmail.com

Paul had to chuckle to himself; if that wasn't a sign then he didn't know what was. He only hoped and prayed that it was the sign. He clicked on the email link. Paul filled in all of the usual boxes.

Name, address, email and phone. He also entered his experience as a psychic medium, a career that he had flourished in and built for more than ten years. He embellished his achievements somewhat. Paul knew he must stand out and be seen. If this was the sign he sought, then Paul must make Sarah Jackson find him.

It was not long; only two days passed before Paul received an answer email from Sarah Jackson. She seemed impressed (as she should) and taken in fully by what he had told her about himself. People were so easy to manipulate if you knew what buttons to press and Paul knew them all. Sarah requested to visit and meet with Paul in person; Paul readily agreed and they set the date for which Sarah was to visit him.

The doorbell rang loudly throughout the house; Paul rose from his chair at the table. Making his way slowly from the sitting room, he was in no rush. He knew who would be at his front door waiting for him and he enjoyed showing his power and making others wait for him. It was a small thing, but still it made Paul feel important, and as long as he felt that way, he was happy.

Paul opened the front door to greet his visitor.

The young woman standing on his porch smiled, looking up at him. "Paul Ackermann?" she asked.

"Yes." Paul looked down at the attractive young lady standing on his porch steps. She looked at him through soft brown eyes. Her hair tied up in a ponytail was swishing in the breeze behind her. To Paul's eyes, she had such a look of young innocence about her. He thought to himself how easy this naïve young girl would be to manipulate and control.

"Hello, I'm Sarah. Sarah Jackson. It is so very good to meet you, Mr Ackermann," Sarah said, extending her hand.

Ignoring the offered hand, Paul replied, "Indeed, it must be a truly wonderful experience for you, my dear. Would you like to come in?"

"Yes, thank you," Sarah said, her hand dropping away to her side as she climbed the steps.

Paul stepped away from the door, holding it wide open so that Sarah could enter. As she passed him, Paul purposely slammed the door closed behind them. Sarah jumped but continued walking, as Paul guided her down the hallway and into the sitting room. He noted how jumpy he made her, something that he could definitely use to his advantage.

Paul gestured for Sarah to take a seat at the table. Once she was settled, Paul slowly walked around the table and sat himself opposite her. Paul's gaze never left Sarah's eyes as he interlocked his fingers and leaned on the table in front of him.

"So, Miss Jackson, you requested this meeting, how may I help you?"

"Please, call me Sarah." Paul gave no acknowledgement. He just sat unmoving and staring. "Well," she continued, his presence putting her slightly on edge and making her feel rather uncomfortable. "As you know from our emails, my partner Tom and I are very impressed with your vast experience and knowledge. I would like to officially offer you a place with us on the team."

Paul remained quiet for several seconds more before he replied. "I see, Sarah. That is indeed a most kind offer to be sure. But you must now appreciate my position. Although I have knowledge and powers most others can only dream of possessing and my skills with the paranormal are unmatched, I do know however very little about you. I would not desire my reputation tarnished by anyone. My speciality you see is not with the living. I would like to learn more about you. Your intentions and experience, for example. Tell me about yourself before I drop everything for your beck and call, and run off to aid you."

Sarah took a deep breath. "Mr Ackermann, please let me first assure you that I, Tom or any of the others on the team would never call and expect you to come running to our summons. We would always try to give you as much notice to upcoming cases as is possible."

"Very well; now Sarah," Paul leaned forward, his gaze penetrating, "tell me about yourself. Tell me about your knowledge of the other side."

Sarah felt awkward, almost naked, before his penetrating gaze. "There…there really isn't much to tell really." Sarah fumbled her way through her sentence, trying to find her confidence. "I have seen a few things that I could not explain through conventional ways. I have seen people that others around me could not. I have heard voices that no one else could, or else they denied hearing them. I do not claim to be an expert on the paranormal; more of an explorer, a seeker of truth. I strongly believe in the afterlife and I want to understand it. I know I'm rambling a bit, I'm still getting used to the idea that there are people out there who don't think me crazy for my beliefs."

Paul for his part seemed completely indifferent to everything Sarah had just told him. Sarah realised that Paul was waiting for her, so she continued.

"I'm sure that in your line of work, Mr Ackermann, you would have experienced, as I have, much scepticism and ridicule over the years. A lot more probably than myself, I would imagine. But let me say, I am no stranger to this ridicule and have been subject to it for much of my life. I…my intention is simply to provide solid evidence to prove the existence of life after death. Therefore, we can provide education and proof to all of the non-believers out there." Sarah paused, waiting for Paul's reaction, waiting for him to say anything.

"Most admirable sentiments, my dear. A crusade, of sorts, for the truth. But I must warn you, and you must surely already know this fact for yourself. The vast majority of people out there will not believe you. They will refuse to believe, no matter what proof you present them with. There are those who will call you a liar and laugh at your so-called proof. They will say that everything you present them with is fake. They will refuse to consider any other possibility than their own version of the truth."

"But don't you see. That's why we're going after hard and irrefutable evidence."

"And tell me, what exactly will you do with your new-found knowledge and power once you have preached to and converted the masses?"

Sarah tried her hardest to ignore Paul's obvious sarcasm. Her voice though began to betray her uneasiness. "I only intend to learn what I can and…and pass that knowledge on. I…I only want to try to educate people, nothing more."

"You do not seek power for yourself?" Paul's eyes narrowed. "You crave nothing beyond the knowledge?" he asked, his voice taut like steel.

Sarah was confused, maybe even a little disturbed by Paul's strange questions. Paul was starting to make her feel very uncomfortable. Where these questions of power came from, she had absolutely no idea. Sarah said as much. "I don't understand your question, Mr Ackermann. Power? I'm sorry, but I really don't understand. The knowledge and proof is all I seek. And quite frankly, no power that I can see other than knowledge can come from any of this. That is my understanding, unless I am missing something."

Paul smiled, a thin-lipped smile as he waved her off. He had her. Sarah had proven herself to be both naive and very easy to control. Paul had more power over Sarah's emotions than she did. The promised power would indeed be his for the taking, thanks to Sarah and her foolish friends. "Yes, as I said, your sentiments are most admirable, my dear Sarah. You may go now, and please, call me when you and your team require my services."

Sarah understood a dismissal when she heard one. In honesty, she was quite pleased to be getting out of the place. Sarah was already regretting inviting this man to join them, but since he was the only person who had responded to her advert, what choice did she have?

Sarah rose from her chair. "Thank you once again for your time and hospitality." She was utterly confused with how the conversation had gone. Sarah struggled to believe that she had even been a contributing part of it. She felt more like she was leaving a tough interrogation room (as the chief suspect) than having offered Paul Ackermann a job. Paul's sudden voice from behind startled Sarah from her thoughts.

"Let me show you the way out, Sarah." Paul took the lead, guiding Sarah to the front door. He opened it wide and gestured for her to exit.

Sarah smiled as she passed Paul, she turned her head forwards again as she trotted down the porch stairs and started across the garden footpath.

"See you again soon, Sarah," Paul called down after her.

"I hope so, and thank you, Mr Ackermann," she replied politely.

"Please, Sarah, please call me Paul."

Finally, some humanity, Sarah thought. She looked back to smile and wave, but Paul had already disappeared inside and slammed the front door shut behind him. Sarah left his property and never looked back. The only thought she had (and not for the first time) was whether or not she had done the right thing bringing Paul onto her team.

Paul returned to his table and sat down in contemplation. He sat thinking about all he had been told by James the previous week. He thought about the sign that had brought Sarah to him. And he thought about what the future would hold for him. *You stupid, pathetic, foolish girl. This will be far too easy. Soon, the power will be mine, and you will all finally accept and respect me. All of those who scorned me will pay dearly. I will see to that.*

Chapter 11
2012 – Sarah and Andrew

Leaving a fuming Paul in the car with Tom and Jessica for the time being, Sarah and Andrew made their way back up to the house.

Sarah walked, deep in thought. She was not so much worried about the house as she was seething with anger regarding Paul.

Sarah had been pretty freaked out for a while after first meeting Paul. It had, however, not taken her very long at all to realise what an egotistical pain in the arse he was. All of his theatrics and posturing were just that—a front, one big act—all to hide the lonely and scared little man that he really was.

Sarah had quickly found out that the best way to deal with and handle Paul was simple. She never backed down and gave him as good as she got. Paul was a bully, and like most bullies, he crumbled when confronted. Since that first time, Sarah had never taken any crap from Paul again. That was something that had, to her delight, greatly annoyed him. Sarah smiled to herself at the memory.

Just ahead of her, Andrew stopped at the front door and turned back to face Sarah. He reached out with his hands and held her gently by her shoulders.

"Sarah, are you totally sure about this?" Andrew asked, the concern clear in his voice.

"Yeah, I had a good scare, and I'll be the first to admit I'm more than a little nervous about going back in. But like you guys said to me, there was nothing to back up what I was saying on film. I don't know, maybe it's like Paul said and I did imagine it. And if I didn't imagine it, who the hell is playing with our equipment? Either way, that's what we're here for. And I tell you now, Andy, I for one ain't going anywhere until I get some damn answers." The old Sarah was back and ready to go.

Andrew smirked at her. "I don't know, now don't get me wrong. What you said happened is not only hard to believe, it's damned near impossible. And with the lack of evidence to back you up, no one will believe a word you say. But if Paul doesn't believe you and wants to dismiss what you said...well, something ain't right.

"Your word against his that something is off is more than good enough for me. I mean, I've known you long enough and you're not the kind of person who makes this shit up. I'm not saying that I'm ready to throw in the towel and become a believer just yet, but if you're game, I'm ready to be convinced, and if you're game to convince me, let's do this."

Andrew pushed the front door open, shining his pencil-thin beam of light from the torch he was carrying on the floor ahead of him and Sarah.

"Well, boss, where to first? You lead the way, I'm right behind you," Andrew said, extinguishing the light.

Sarah led the way. "Come on. Let's check out the sitting room first."

They entered the sitting room. Sarah took the big overstuffed armchair whilst Andrew stretched out comfortably on the sofa.

"Okay, Andy," Sarah said. Her voice was slightly shaky, nerves from her earlier ordeal. "If you just listen for a while, I'm going to do some EVP work; if you hear any responses or see anything, let me know. Okay?"

"I'm all ears."

Sarah switched on her portable night vision digital camera, adjusting the flip screen so she could see around the room. She got herself comfortable in the chair, took a deep breath and began.

"Is there anyone here in this place with us? Don't be afraid, we aren't here to hurt you. We just want to meet you and say hello. My name is Sarah and this is my good friend Andrew."

"Hello."

"Are you here watching us? Can you give us a sign? Can you touch one of us or move something?"

Nothing happened, all was quiet.

"Do you want us here? Do you want us to go? If you want us to go then you will have to give us a sign."

Sarah panned her camera around the room—nothing. She strained her ears—nothing. Andrew sat up fast. "Did you hear that?"

"What?" Sarah's nerves flared.

"I thought I heard someone knocking on the wall behind us."

Sarah turned her head and camera in the direction Andrew thought he heard the noise coming from. Nothing.

"Are you sure you heard something? I mean, could it have been outside?"

"Look, Sarah, I know what you went through earlier and you know what I think of this paranormal stuff. There is no way I would make it up so, no. No way would I do that to you. It was definitely inside this room."

"Okay well, let's try again, I know we have all night but I would love to hear and capture something definite. Was that you? Did you knock on the wall? If you did, thank you. Can you do it again or can you do it closer? Can you knock on this table? Like this."

Sarah was back in control now, she leaned forwards and knocked gently on the table with her knuckles. Tap…tap. Nothing.

"Can you copy me?" Tap…tap. Nothing.

"Sarah, if you don't mind, can I try something?" Andrew asked.

"Sure, go for it."

"What's the matter, you chicken shit or something?" Sarah winced. Andrew continued.

"What's up, huh? You can scare women and kids when they're on their own, but you hide when we get here together. I know why you can't tap or knock, you can't, can you? You're weak, ain't ya? Can't do shit. You some kind of sick and weak pervert who's too damn scared to show themsel—" BANG!

The coffee table visibly moved several inches.

"Holy fucking shit. Did you get that, Sarah?" Andrew shouted.

"No, no, I didn't. I hope the stationary camera did though. That was amazing. Shit. Oh shit."

"Yeah, this is awesome. Tell you what, all those stupid shows on television Jess made me sit through, I thought was all bullshit. But this, wow. That table just fucking moved all by itself."

Andrew swung his legs off and sat up straight on the sofa, fully alert. Listening, watching.

"What the hell, Andy, where the hell did you learn that, I mean what on earth made you think to talk to it like that?"

Andrew shrugged.

"Well, if I'm honest with you, it was one of the shows I said about. Don't get me wrong. Most of them were, are, complete crap and they believed anything and tried to make the viewer believe anything. But there was one, some

American show where the teams would go to these places and do everything they could to debunk the haunting claims. And they only admitted to a real haunting when they had conclusive proof.

"Kind of like what you're trying to do, that was the only one I didn't mind. Ghost Hunters I think it was called, or something like that. I saw one of them do that once, they gave it some real attitude and made it so angry that they got a response. You gotta admit. It beats the old sitting around a table, moving a glass with your finger and telling the gullible audience it was a ghost moving it. Bollocks. But these guys, I hate to admit it but they were the real deal. And guess what? It just bloody worked."

Sarah nodded, shaking slightly. It was caused partly through nerves and partly through the excitement.

"Okay, Andy, that was cool. Let me try again."

"It's all yours."

"Who are you? Thank you for banging on and moving the table for us. Can you do anything else? Can you make a noise with your voice? Andrew does not really believe you're here. If you don't do anything else, he will dismiss what you did. Are you Julia? Are you the woman who killed her sister?"

Ha ha ha ha.

"Fuck me." Andrew was on his feet. "Tell me you heard that? That was bloody laughter." Sarah was grinning from ear to ear.

"I did. But, Andy, that didn't sound like a woman to me. It was too deep. I think it was a man.

"Was that you, Robert Castleleigh? Did you work for the lord? Who are you?"

Sarah continued to scan the camera around the room as both she and Andrew listened intently. Nothing.

"Enough of this shit. If you're here then do something else and prove it. Did you die here or did you murder someone here? Is that the best you can do? Pathetic, I'm not impressed at all. All you can do is move a table and laugh, wow. Come on scare us, do something," Andrew challenged.

Nothing.

They sat still, listening for several minutes before Sarah broke the silence. "I don't think it's going to happen again Andrew, come on, let's get out of here and try upstairs." Sarah stood up and walked out the door, using the night vision on her camera to see the way.

Andrew followed her out, properly excited for the first time on the investigation, but disappointed that nothing else had happened. He halted behind Sarah at the bottom of the staircase, gently holding her arm.

"What do you think, Sarah, really? Who do you think it was?" he asked uncertainly.

"Honestly, I don't know, but I'm positive it was a man. That voice, that laughter? It couldn't have been a woman, it was too deep, wasn't it?"

"So what, you reckon it's that lord thingy or the guy that worked for him? Maybe even that Pembleton character?"

"I don't know, Andrew; I hate to say it, but maybe if Paul was here, he could answer that."

The sitting room door slammed shut behind them, causing them to physically jump as they spun around towards the noise.

"Shit, Sarah, this is getting real. How the hell did that door shut all on its own? Jesus, it's been wide open all this time and it chooses this moment to close? I'm meant to be the bloody sceptic here. We've been back in here, what? Ten minutes and I'm ready to take it all back, I'm a believer," he said breathlessly.

"Amazing, isn't it," Sarah said. "Who would have thought that we would have so much activity so soon? I'm gonna go get Paul, I think we really do need him if we're gonna find out just exactly who or what is in here messing with us."

"Okay, Sarah but watch him, yeah, I don't trust the guy."

"Me neither, but this is all happening too damn fast for me. We…I need help." She started to head for the front door.

"Sarah?" Andrew called quietly after her.

She stopped and looked over her shoulder at him. "Yeah?"

"Don't be too long, okay."

She smirked to herself. "Don't you worry, mister non-believer, I won't leave you alone in this spooky house for long."

Without another word, Sarah walked to the front door, opened it and stepped outside. The door shut firmly behind her on its own with a slightly nervous Andrew still inside.

You need to get out.

"What the fuck!" Andrew whispered, spinning around.

I do not have much time. You must leave, you are in danger if you stay here.

Andrew turned on the spot several times, searching the darkness for the origin of the voice. His whole body shook and broke out in goosebumps whilst the hairs on his hands, arms and neck stood fully erect.

"Who…who's there?" Andrew stammered, trying to keep his voice steady.

Nothing.

"Talk to me, dammit, what do you want?" His voice betrayed an equal mixture of nerves and agitation.

I can control William for now, but my power will fade when James returns. Please heed me, you must go. Now.

The voice was flat and held no emotion, yet Andrew sensed the underlying urgency all the same. "We can't leave," he tried to explain as if having a normal everyday conversation. "We have to find out what is going on here for the family. They're terrified and we're here trying to help them. Who is this, William? Who are you?"

Nothing.

Andrew was on the verge of either bolting for the nearest exit or calling out again when the front door abruptly opened, scaring him half to death as Sarah and Paul entered the hallway.

"Jesus shit, you just scared the crap outta me. You aren't gonna believe what just happened. Hell, I can hardly believe it myself."

Sarah touched his shaking arm. "What's up, Andrew?" Even in the dark, the only illumination coming from the camera, she could see and feel the nervousness radiating outwards from him.

"I think I'm either completely mad or I have developed one hell of an imagination. You won't believe this, Sarah, but I just had a conversation with a woman."

Sarah was taken aback, a confession like this from a total sceptic like Andrew was nothing short of amazing. If it had been anyone else, she would have sought proof, but somehow, being Andrew, she believed him. Unfortunately, other people would demand proof and that was, after all, what they were searching for.

"That's fantastic, Andrew. Did you get it on your recorder?"

"Shit no. I'm sorry, Sarah, I didn't even think about it. It was just so strange, you know? It was like she was stood right next to me but all around at once as well. Freaky, huh?"

Sarah nodded, more to herself than Andrew. She was trying to watch Paul, as he shined his torch around the hallway as if he were looking for something or someone. He turned back to Andrew. "Did you actually see this alleged person?" he asked abruptly.

"No, like I said it was just this voice. Definitely female though."

"Curious, this woman obviously has strong energies if she can talk to you. Tell me, what exactly did she say?" Paul asked slowly, his tone clearly showing his interest.

"It was a warning, she said we had to get out because we are in danger."

"And did this mystery woman happen to actually tell you what the so-called danger we face is? Did she tell you who she is or happen to mention any names? In short, is there anything useful at all you can tell me?"

Andrew was somewhat taken aback by Paul's indifferent attitude towards his experience. "No, Paul, I have no idea who she is, was, whatever. But she did mention the name William." Being dark, nobody noticed Paul's body stiffen slightly at the mention of the name William.

Andrew continued, oblivious.

"She said something about that she was controlling him, but that she wouldn't be able to when James returned."

"James? What, not Pembleton?" Sarah gasped, remembering what she had been told and read about, not to mention her possible earlier experience with that evil man.

"I don't know. I really don't. She said this and then was gone. That was when you two came back in and scared the shit out of me. What do you make of all this, Paul?" Andrew asked, personal feelings aside in a hope that the man could help him understand what was happening.

"Interesting. This woman seems to think, and in fact told you as much, that William is dangerous. Yet consider this. It is by her own admission, as you said, she who controls him. I must tell you though, and I feel that it is important to mention this to you both, I spoke to a gentleman named William earlier. It was earlier this evening when I was actually permitted to be in the house, when you were setting up the equipment." The sarcasm almost dripped from Paul's lips.

He continued, "I can tell you now with utter confidence that he is, in fact, a perfect gentleman. William was an innocent man who was brutally murdered by a woman. Most probably I expect the same one that you now claim to have spoken to, Andrew. I can tell you honestly, you have no more to fear from

William than you do from me. No, I suspect it is this woman that you should be wary of. I would say to you, beware the false prophets."

Sarah was not at all comforted or convinced by Paul's statement. She seemed to be both confused and angry at his words; if anything, her level of distrust for Paul rose. She shone the camera's light on Paul.

"What, when? You knew this and didn't tell us? Damn it, Paul, we're supposed to be a team. You should have told us all this earlier; we need...we have to know what it is we are up against. That is why you're here after all. Now, is there anything else you forgot to mention and want to share with us?"

Paul sighed at her dramatics. "No, there is nothing else you need to know. You really must learn to trust me, Sarah. I am not the novice here. Please try to remember that. Now come." He smiled. "Let us head upstairs and see if we can find Henry."

If Sarah had a gasket, she would have blown it at that point. She stared daggers at Paul.

"Who the fuck is Henry? Someone else you may have forgotten to tell us about? You want us to trust you, Paul, fine, but it's a two-way street. Give us a reason why we should," she shouted at him.

"Please, Sarah, calm down. There really is no need to become quite so hysterical." He patted the air with the palms of his hands. "I haven't told you everything for your own good. You are still young and very inexperienced in these sensitive things, that much has been clear to me since our first meeting. Now please calm down for a moment and let me explain to you what I know about Henry."

Sarah could not help but want to shout and call Paul an egotistical, chauvinistic, condescending, pretentious prick. She decided to hold her tongue though, deciding a full-blown argument could wait until later when this was over. Andrew however could not help himself, self-restraint had never been his strongest suit.

"Paul, do you have to be such a first-class twat? Now stop being such a wanker, say what you got to say or get the fuck out. You talk to Sarah like that again and you'll be on your arse." Paul for his part completely ignored Andrew's outburst and continued talking.

"Henry is a deeply evil man, when he was alive, he brutally and without any hint of mercy killed his master and his master's young daughter too. He is the one we must be wary, very wary of. The others here in this place refer to him as the Splitting Man. And he, I cannot stress this point enough to you, he is very dangerous."

Andrew was not convinced, but held his tongue this time. It was, after all, him and Jessica who had done the research on the whole area. The woman that he had spoken to had seemed totally on the level to him, and if William was indeed the innocent that Paul made him out to be, then why would he and James Pembleton be together?

If the James that the woman referred to really was James Pembleton…no, something was not right. Neither Andrew or Jessica had found any reference to any other man named James during their research. Paul was lying to them for some reason. Andrew was convinced of it. He could not prove anything yet so kept his thoughts to himself, for now. But he would be watching Paul very closely from now on.

Paul shone his torch one last time down at the sitting room door and smiled. Andrew and Sarah never noticed his smile, which was just as well. He would have hated to have to explain why he was so happy to see James Pembleton holding a struggling Julia down on the floor by her throat. Looking above him at the stairs once more, Paul started to climb as he followed a beckoning William. Sarah and Andrew followed, oblivious to the evil presences mounting all around them.

Once at the top, Paul made a beeline straight for the parents' bedroom. He crossed to the dresser, pulled the blanket from the mirror and dramatically tossed it on the bed. He looked deep into the glass and watched as Sarah and Andrew came into the room behind him.

Andrew was sure that he had removed the blanket covering the mirror earlier when he was setting the equipment up, but decided not to say anything about it. He couldn't help sniping though.

"I guess we're following his lead now?" Andrew agitatedly whispered in Sarah's ear.

"Let's just go with it for now, okay?" she whispered back, trying to keep Andrew calm.

She moved to stand next to Paul so that both of their reflections were visible to Andrew in the mirror.

"So, Paul," he called out. "What are we doing in here then? What's your plan?"

"Andrew, have you ever heard of scrying before?" Paul asked, turning around.

"No, should I have?"

"I am not surprised. However, with your experience downstairs still fresh, you may actually be the perfect person to attempt this. If, that is, you are willing to do so."

"Well, how about telling me what the hell scrying is, and I will tell you if I'm willing to do it or not." The hostility he felt towards Paul was very clear in his voice.

"Okay, listen carefully and you may just learn something. Scrying is a means of seeing or communicating with the other side through a physical medium. We can use several things for mediums in which to scry through. You could use something as simple as glass of water or a crystal. Obviously, even you would have heard of crystal balls. For us though, I think the mirror here would prove best. Mirrors are used very widely for scrying. And when we consider what Mrs Phillips has already claimed to see in this very mirror, well, I think we have a great chance at success."

Andrew grinned. "Okay, so you want me to use the mirror as a crystal ball and tell you what's in your future?"

Shaking his head and trying to ignore Andrew's obvious sarcasm and baiting, Paul continued, "Please, Andrew, please try to pay attention to what I am telling you. Scrying is a very powerful way to communicate with those that have passed on, but it can also be extremely dangerous for the scryer. Let me explain how it works exactly. Now, you will be required to sit with the mirror in front of you. You must clear your mind of everything except that which you wish to achieve.

"You must concentrate on finding who is here in the house with us and nothing else. You may call out and use your voice but your eyes must never leave the surface of the mirror. Now, when I say look into the mirror, what I mean is you must look beyond it. You must not focus on any one thing but try to look beyond the mirror, seeing everything and nothing all the same time.

"Visions will come to you and you may see various things, they can happen in different ways but I will not tell you what. This way, it will help Sarah gather her precious evidence correctly. You will tell us what you see after the event. A word of warning though, you may see all sorts of strange things. You may see things from the past, from the present or yes, even from the future. I warn you though, do not get yourself too caught up in what you see. When you have seen enough, you must turn away or close your eyes. Do not risk getting stuck with what you see. Do you understand all that I have told you?"

Andrew came forwards and sat on the stall by the dresser. He looked up at Paul, his face a mask of seriousness. "Okay, I will give it a go. But how will I know if it works or not?"

"Trust me, Andrew, you will know."

"That's what I'm afraid of. Okay, so where will you guys be whilst I'm doing this scrying thing?"

"I think it's probably best that we split up. I would suggest that I try and get to the bottom of what is happening in the bathroom. Obviously, Sarah had a most traumatic experience in there earlier, so I will not be so insensitive as to ask you to join me."

He turned to face Sarah. "Sarah, it may pay for you to go and have a lie down on the girl's bed as Jessica did earlier. Try calling out, try to make some form of contact. If you have need of my assistance, just call and I will come immediately to you. Do not worry, Andrew; if you need assistance, you only have to call out. Sarah and I will not be far."

Andrews's eyes narrowed as he listened uncertainly to Paul's words, but it was Sarah who beat him to the punch this time.

"Paul, I think it is time for complete honesty here. What the hell is going on?"

"Whatever do you mean, Sarah?" Paul asked; he seemed genuinely taken aback.

"Okay, let's start with this. Downstairs, you pretty much dismissed everything that Andrew said about this woman he spoke to. Then you were in a rush to get us up here, you said that you wanted to find someone called Henry, whom you claimed was evil. Now all you want to do is split us up. Why?"

Paul was blatantly uncomfortable with Sarah's outburst, but was determined to do things his way, in his time. How dare this slip of a girl presume to question him? But he knew that he must keep their trust if everything was to work out as he had planned. He wanted everything to be perfect before he sprung his trap on them.

"Very well, Sarah, if you really do think that you are owed and deserve an explanation, then I will do my best to accommodate you. It is very simple. Yes, I do want to find Henry, but he is simply not here at the moment. I am a spiritual medium, not a magician. You see, nothing sinister is going on. But it is up to you; we can sit here together and wait for him to appear to us or for something else to happen. Or we can get proactive and actually try to bring out the beings that are here."

"I hate to side with him, Sarah, but he does have a point. We came here to do a job. I guess the ghosts here don't have a timetable so it really is up to us to try and get their attention."

Paul smiled, having Andrew on side meant certain victory. Sarah would, he knew, crumble to his will now.

"Fine." Sarah was not happy. "Andrew, you're right," She sighed at having to give in and submit to Paul. "But we all stay on the same floor. If any of us call for help, the others must stop what they are doing and come help the other. And I mean straight away, Paul, is that clear?"

"Perfectly; now, Andrew. If you please, could you turn to face the mirror? Good, now look into and past the glass. Can you see the light from the camera behind you?"

"Yes, why?"

"Do not look at it. You are looking too far, use the light to see but try to look only five or six inches beyond the mirror and no more. Now concentrate, you must decide who you wish to contact."

"That's easy, the woman from earlier."

"No," Paul almost screamed; he recovered quickly and continued in his normal voice, "No, Andrew, that could be very dangerous for you. You are a beginner at this and therefore, you must start small. To begin with, I think that you should just try and find William. If you can do that, he may be willing to help and guide you."

"Fine," Andrew huffed, looking at Sarah. "But I keep blinking; is that a problem?"

"No, you may blink normally. Just do your best and try to make sure that you do not lose focus. I will be in the bathroom."

Paul turned and left the room, leaving Andrew and Sarah alone.

"Andrew, listen," Sarah whispered. "I don't trust him anymore than you do. Something is definitely wrong here. I really don't think this William that Paul was talking about is the one we should talk to. At least not yet, and certainly not until we get a clearer picture of what the hell is really going on around here."

"Yeah, I was thinking the same thing. Despite what that moron said, I'm going to try and contact that woman again. Maybe it is Julia and I'm putting myself in danger. I don't know and I really can't explain it, but I just got the feeling she wanted to help us. What are you going to do?"

"Me? I'm going to do just what Paul said," Sarah said innocently with a sly smile.

Shocked, Andrew turned around in his seat, looking at Sarah through the gloom as if she had just gone mad. "But you just said…"

"I know what I said, and I meant it. I don't trust him as far as I could throw him. Listen Andrew, if this William and James Pembleton are communicating with Paul, then this could be really bad. Two spirits, both from different times. If I'm right, then that is wrong and can't be good for us. Paul said this Henry was the evil one, but I tell you, Andrew, I'm not convinced by anything that weasel tells us. So, I'm going to go and lie on Alice's bed and try to talk to this Henry if I can. I think he's the one who stands over Alice. I don't know why, and maybe I'm way off the mark, but I've just got this feeling. I think it's like he watches over her, protecting her or something."

"Sarah, are you sure about this? What if we have this all wrong and Paul really is on the level after all?" She could hear the concern in his voice as he searched her eyes for understanding.

"Yes, I'm sure. If it goes wrong, what's the worst that can happen? But I have a strong feeling that I'm not wrong. If there is one thing I have learned in my life, Andrew, it's to trust my instincts."

"Okay, but go careful. I'm only here if I need you."

"You mean, if I need you?"

Andrew smiled. "Just keep your ears open, I will too. Now go on, get out, I've got some scrying to get on with," he said in his best imitation of Paul.

Sarah left the room, making sure that she left the door wide open, and crossed the hall to enter Alice's bedroom. She climbed on the bed, lay back and got herself comfortable. Pulling the digital recorder from her pocket, she turned it on and placed it by her hip. Sarah turned on the camera too, putting it on her stomach, resting her hands close by.

Okay, here goes nothing, Sarah thought to herself. She took a few deep breaths, calming and preparing herself. Then she began.

"Is there anyone in this room with me?" she called out, gently but firmly. "Can you hear me? Can you make a sound or knock on something?" Nothing.

"I know you're here, Alice has told us about you. Is that why you won't show yourself, because I'm not Alice? She is scared of you and asked me to help her. I only want to talk to you. Please, if you are here can yo…"

Sarah slowly sat up; she picked up the camera and panned around the room. "I just heard footsteps approaching the bed, they…they have stopped now. Whatever it is, it's stood right next to the bed. Right next to me. Are you here? Is that you standing next to my bed? Is it you, Henry?"

Pretty lady.

Sarah almost jumped out of her skin at the sound of the deep, thunderous voice right next to where she sat. "Thank…thank you," she said, trying to control her breathing. "My name is Sarah, what is your name?"

Nothing.

"Come on, please talk to me." Sarah tried to keep her voice sounding calm and spoke slowly, but she was struggling in the excitement of the contact. "I promise I won't hurt you. I just want to talk to you. I'm here to help the family that lives here. Do you like them, do you protect them?…Henry?"

You not hurt?

Sarah could not believe it. She had finally made contact with a spirit and she was actually talking to one. She had to try and maintain her composure. "No, I will not hurt anyone. You wouldn't hurt me, would you?" she asked, almost nervously.

No, I look after.

"Who do you look after?"

My friend, Molly. She made me go. I didn't want to, but she made me.

"Did you protect her?"

I tried, she sent Henry away. Edward come back, he kill Miss Molly and Master.

Sarah checked the red recording light was on. *This is incredible. I'm getting all this and he just confirmed his identity to me*, she thought. "Does Molly live here, Henry?"

No. Miss Molly dead.

"Who did you say killed her, Henry? Who killed Molly?" Sarah knew that she was on the verge of understanding.

Edward kill her. Master kill him for making Molly. Edward come back to kill Molly and Master.

"Who is the master, Henry?"

Casly, Lord Casly.

Casly, who the hell is Casly? Then it hit her.

"Lord Castleleigh, he was your master, Henry?"

Yes, he kill Edward. He kill Henry.

"Why did he kill you, Henry? I was told it was you who killed Molly and Lady Castleleigh," Sarah said in confusion.

No. The voice denied. *Henry no kill no one. Her lady, she fall and die. Henry blamed and got killed. Henry stay to protect Miss Molly from others, but she send Henry away. Edward come, he kill Lord Casly and Miss Molly.*

Sarah could almost hear the voice sob as he spoke sadly of Molly's death. She felt for this Henry, but Sarah needed to understand and make sense of it all. "Henry, you said Edward killed Molly. Why would he do that?"

He make Molly with the lady.

It slowly started to make sense to Sarah, and proved that history could not always be trusted. Or, at least, those who wrote history couldn't always be trusted. She realised that Henry had not killed Lord Castleleigh and his daughter, but this other. This Edward, who apparently seemed to have had an affair with Lady Castleleigh, was the one responsible for their deaths. The child Molly was his daughter, not the lord's. She could not make sense of why he would kill his own child though.

"Henry, why did Edward kill Molly?"

Her fault, he say. Her fault that he got found out and made to be dead.

"Thank you so much for talking to me, Henry. I would like to ask you a few more questions, if that is okay?"

Nothing.

Sarah took the silence for a yes, so she carried on. "Henry, do you know the others who are here in this place? People who may have died, but still remain here?"

Bad men.

"Do you protect the family that lives here now, Henry?"

Henry like Alice. I look after her. William no hurt her when Henry here. Henry won't let him.

Sarah stiffened at the mention of William's name, the second time she had heard his name in a bad light. "Does William want to hurt her, Henry?"

Him and his friend, they want to hurt them but can't.

"That's good that they can't, is it because you're here to protect the family and stop them, Henry?"

Yes, we protect. But no more, they gone now. William and his friends want you now.

Sarah blinked several times. A feeling of dread began to descend on her. The temperature suddenly and very noticeably dropped by several degrees. Sarah broke out in goosebumps and she started to shake with the news that she was hearing. The people who wanted to hurt her were the very same people that Paul told her, just a few minutes previous, that he wanted her to try and contact.

Bastard, she thought.

The bed creaked as the mattress sank next to where she sat, it felt to her as if someone was sitting down next to her.

"Henry, why do they want to hurt us?" Sarah asked quietly; she was growing afraid of the knowledge she was gaining. Sarah found herself being gently pulled back, her head gently resting against a massive muscular chest. Her hair was being caressed as was her shoulder. It was not hands and fingers that caressed her, but stumps stroking against her. Sarah was strangely not scared or repulsed by this but actually comforted by the ghostly giant that held her protectively.

They like to hurt. We help you.

"We, who is we, Henry?" Sarah asked softly.

Julia, she stop William before. She my friend here. We help you, Sarah. You safe with Henry. They can no hurt you when Henry here.

Andrew, she almost jumped of the bed. "Henry, we have to warn Andrew and Paul. We have to go out and tell the others."

No. Henry protect Sarah.

"We have to, Henry, they're my friends. If they're in danger, I must help them."

No, not him. Paul bad man. Paul and William friends.

The door to Alice's room shut quietly with a firm click.

As Sarah left the room, Andrew slowly turned his attention back to the mirror. He tried, as Paul had instructed him, to clear his mind as he thought of nothing but the woman's voice who had spoken to him earlier. He stared into the mirror's depths as he concentrated his vision. Andrew hated doing what Paul said, but for Sarah, he was willing to try.

"Can you hear me?" he whispered. "You tried to talk to me earlier, you told me we were in danger. Please talk to me now if you can. We are here only to help, but we can't help you unless you speak to us."

A fine mist began to form in his line of sight. Andrew stiffened slightly in his seat, but he was determined to remain focussed. He refused to look away. Slowly, the mist cleared until he could see a man about his own age standing behind him. The man looked normal, that is to say, he was not see-through and wispy like your stereotypical ghost. He was solid as he stood looking straight back at Andrew.

"Are you real? Am I really seeing you?" Andrew asked, a little unnerved and unsure of himself, not sure whether to scream or not.

Define real? Am I here with you? Yes. Am I dead? From your point of view, yes.

"Who are you? I spoke to a woman earlier, who was she?"

She cannot come, she used too much energy when she spoke to you and now James has her. There is a great evil here, you should have listened to her and heeded her warning, Andrew. You should have gone whilst you had the chance.

"We can't go yet. We have to know what is happening here," Andrew said. More certain than ever that he had to try after hearing that last statement.

Very well, if you cannot be persuaded by me to leave, then I will show you. Continue to look at the mirror and I shall show you everything you need to know. I am sorry, but you must be warned, what you need to see is not necessarily what you want to see. It will not be nice, but it is necessary, observe, Andrew.

Andrew sat still, silent. He gave no indication whether he had heard the warning or not as he continued to gaze deep into the glass of the mirror. The man behind him disappeared. He could now see a big man chopping wood in a field next to a huge manor house. The images changed and flashed like a kaleidoscope through his mind as he witnessed Lady Castleleigh's accidental death and Henry dying at Lord Castleleigh's hands.

He watched as the lord himself and his daughter were brutally slain and butchered in their own home by another man. A man dressed very similar to Henry, but without a doubt not him. The name Edward came to him.

The images changed, he saw the sadistic William as he tortured and danced around whilst he killed Emily Farrow. Andrew did not know how the names came to him, but he just knew them to be right. He watched as a devastated Julia, too late to save her sister, took William's life.

Andrew cried openly, tears racing down his cheeks as he watched an ill Catherine kill her children, and recognised her husband Oliver as the man who had spoken to him. He watched Oliver die inside from the understanding of the tragedy that had befallen his family. Andrew watched as Oliver burnt his house and family, reuniting them in death.

He watched as James Pembleton viciously beat and killed woman after woman. He watched as James finally met his match in Karen and died in agony, drowning in his own blood. He saw Sarah as she sat on a bed talking to Henry and later, as she lay safe in his protective embrace. Andrew had no scientific evidence or proof, but somehow, he knew that everything he could see was both real, and the truth.

He saw Paul sat on the toilet in the bathroom talking to James Pembleton and William. He heard them planning his, Andrew's, death and the capture and death of Sarah. They talked about how they would lure Tom and Jessica inside the house and murder them too. They spoke of 'veils' and ultimate powers. Andrew heard the talk of higher beings as they sat and planned his own and the death of his friends.

Andrew was mesmerised by all he saw and could not look away from the mirror now, even if he had wanted to.

The bedroom door shut quietly behind an oblivious Andrew as he continued to sit and stare, trance-like, at the mirror and the flashing images of things past, present and future before him.

Two men, one very smartly dressed and a scruffy-looking man now stood behind Andrew.

Andrew watched as Paul entered the room and, with a large glass paperweight, smashed him in the head time and time again. He hit Andrew until his head was unrecognisable and the paperweight dripped blood and gore. A single strand of bloody hair fell from his caved-in head. It landed on the dresser in front of Andrew, startling him back to reality.

Andrew gasped. He was out of breath and sweating as he placed his hands on the dresser for support. Drawing in huge lungful of air, he tried to understand and make sense of everything that he had seen. Did he imagine Oliver? How could he have, it seemed so real. He had seen and witnessed so much, everything that had gone on in this area. He knew the truth. He knew and understood the lies.

Sarah was safe for now, he knew. She was safe whilst she remained with Henry.

Paul. He had to get to the others and warn them of Paul!

"Hello, Andrew, James here tells me you have been busy. Tell me, you foolish non-believer, tell me everything that you saw."

Andrew looked daggers at Paul and began to rise to his feet when suddenly, he could not move. He looked to either side and was more than a little startled to see William holding him firm by his left arm and James by his right. "Why?" he asked nervously. "Why, Paul?"

Paul moved in close, his nose inches from Andrew's own. "Why? You ask me why? Let me tell you why. It is because of people like you, Andrew, people who are too blind to see as I do. It is only now, at the end, that you finally open your eyes to the possibilities. People who doubt and call me names like fake or con artist. I am neither of these things, as you can now see. I am the real deal.

"People like you walk around all the time, blind to the possibilities. You cannot see those things that are right in front of you, as I can. You, Sarah and the others tried to use me for your own ends. You wanted to use me to get your five minutes of fame. Well, now, the tables have turned and my friends here have aided me. They use my energies and now your energies too as they come closer to our world, closer to the crossing. We have an understanding, you see, they love to cause pain and suffering. They love to kill, and I love to talk to and help the dead. I will talk to you again soon, Andrew."

Andrew struggled in vain against his captors as Paul turned his back on him and walked over to the shelves. Paul picked up a large glass paperweight and began studying its coloured patterns. Andrew recognised the ornament from his vision; he was terrified.

"Paul, please, you don't have to do this. Sarah was your friend, how could you do this? We trusted you."

Paul casually walked back to Andrew. "You never did. I could always feel your damn accusing eyes on me. I suppose you were the sensible one not to trust me. No longer though will I have to put up with your hurtful taunts, Andrew."

Paul raised his arm, holding the paperweight high above his head. He grinned then, an evil deranged grin as he brought the paperweight smashing down upon Andrew's head. Paul felt the skull give with the impact. He smashed it over and over. Andrew's head collapsed in upon itself with the repeated pounding until it was nothing but a bloody crater upon his shoulders.

Paul opened his hand and dropped the bloody paperweight, watching it as it thumped to the carpeted floor and began to roll, leaving a thin scarlet trail behind it.

Andrew fell, no longer supported by the spirits of James and William, dead to the floor.

"Andrew, Andrew. Quick, you must come with me. We can't let them take you."

"Oliver?" Andrew looked at the man, he had absolutely no idea what was happening to him.

Oliver took a confused Andrew by the arm. He pulled and dragged Andrew to his feet. Together, they ran from the room, down the stairs and into the sitting room where Andrew saw Julia sat on the sofa, patiently waiting for them.

"I think we have some talking and explaining to do," Emily Farrow said to Andrew.

Paul turned to face James. "Well, that was fun," he said as he looked down at the bloody and unrecognisable mess that was once Andrew. "You were quite right, having the power over someone else's life is most invigorating. Now, are you sure this will work?"

Of course I am sure, the apparition of James said. *Once you have lured those other two fools inside and helped us kill them, then we will have the power to finally destroy Henry. We will use the energies from Sarah so we may gain more power and continue to murder the living with no fear of repercussions. You have our thanks but we ask one more favour of you.*

"Name it, my friend," Paul replied, full of his own importance.

When their whole crew is dead except for Sarah, we want you to be our hands. You will be instrumental in her death. You will be the final ingredient. You will be the one who makes this all possible for us. Now go, we have disabled their cameras as before when I had fun in the bath with Sarah. They will be seeing nothing of what is truly happening. Now, you must fetch the other two living ones before they become suspicious and aware of what is happening. We must take them by surprise.

Paul rushed off to bring Tom and Jessica inside, never once pausing to question his own safety and assurance of life.

William said, "We will deal with that imbecile later." He and James left the room and the dead body of Andrew. They crossed the hall and stood outside of Alice's bedroom. William knocked loudly on the door.

Open up, Henry, your time is up. We want her.

William placed his hand upon the doorknob and began to turn it.

Chapter 12
1749-2012 – The Voice

"Andrew, please sit down," Emily said, motioning to the sofa beside her.

"What…what is going on here?" Andrew asked as he took in the room and its occupants. Emily, who he had mistaken for Julia, sat on the sofa watching him. Catherine stood behind the sofa. Oliver, who was still next to Andrew, walked away, he moved around to stand with his wife.

"I will explain everything to you, Andrew, but please sit with me. It is okay, you are not in any immediate danger. They cannot enter here. This is our place."

"I have to get out," Andrew said, staring at them all in complete disbelief. His eyes danced from one to the other. "I have to warn Jess and Tom. I have to get Sarah out," Andrew said desperately, as his legs started to fail him. He sat down heavily on the sofa next to Emily, his head hung in his hands.

"Andrew, listen to me," Emily said, placing her hand on his back. "For the time being, Sarah is safe. And she will remain so. Whilst she remains with Henry, they cannot hurt her. As for your sister and Tom, they are safe outside. It is what happens here, inside, that must concern us. There is an explanation that is long overdue, and I will do my best to give it to you. But first, I have to ask you, Andrew. Do you understand your position?"

"My position?" Andrew's hands dropped as he looked up into Emily's kind face, searching it for understanding.

"Do you understand what happened to you before, when you were upstairs?"

"Yes, Paul attacked me. He hit me with something," Andrew's hand found the top of his head as it searched for devastating wounds that should have been there. Andrew's hand found no evidence of injury.

"Andrew, you're dead."

Silence followed as a single sad tear escaped the corner of Andrew's eye. He wiped it away with his fingertips and closed his eyes. Nodding slowly and taking in a deep shuddering breath, "I know," he whispered, his lips barely moving enough to let the words out. "I know. But why? It is strange, but I have already accepted it as the truth. Is that wrong? Shouldn't I be shouting and screaming in denial or something?" Andrew asked softly.

Emily smiled at him. "Andrew, that is a big misconception, I do not know where it came from. Most likely from the living, but when you are dead, you are dead. You know by pure human instincts when you are alive, why then should death be any different? Your time in the realm of the living is over, and it is now time to start your next step.

"It really is that simple; as humans, we have the power of mind to accept it. But just because we are dead, it does not mean that we always have to disappear and move on to His world as many of the living would have you believe. Some do, it is true, but for the vast majority of the dead, it is left to the individual to choose.

"If we feel we have things left to do, then, and if He wills it, we may stay. We can move on later if we achieve this and so desire. But again, it is mostly, but not always, our choice. There are, from time to time, occasions when He asserts His will and commands us.

"I…we here have a very important job to do. I was murdered. Catherine and Oliver have their own story, but they too stayed to help. My own sister, Julia, killed herself. But she too remains to watch over the living with us. We were all chosen by Him, chosen to become His champions against the evil. We are the protectors of the innocent. We love the living and will do whatever we can within our power to protect them. You know how we all died, I believe. You saw it in the mirror?"

Andrew nodded. "But why am I here? I was given no choice to stay here or go anywhere; I just am."

Emily smiled. "With our help, Andrew, you shall learn the answers that you seek. Have faith."

All the talk of death and afterlife, seeking answers and having faith had Andrew shaken. He had never been a man of faith and had little in the way of belief, but with everything happening, Andrew was prepared to listen.

"Okay, let us tell you what happened after our deaths. We will tell you of the voice, of what happened to bring us all together to this point now. It all started long ago with Henry. But Henry was not the first; he was however the first of us that the voice recruited. He would tell you himself but he is busy. As you know, he remains with and protects Sarah as we speak. You must understand everything, Andrew, or we will never be able to defeat them. They will win and that is something that we cannot afford to let happen to this world."

"But why do I need to know? Can't we just get Sarah out and send the others away?"

"It is not that simple, Andrew; prophesied events are fast coming to a head, events that were set into motion long ago. Please try to understand that it is extremely hard for us to communicate with the living, hence we cannot just tell your friends to leave. But that is only a small part of the greater problem. They, the dark one's champions, are getting far stronger than they should be and are doing far more than just communicating. I get ahead of myself."

Andrew was confused. "What is, I don't—"

"Please, Andrew, do not talk just try to listen and understand what I tell you. I will tell you Henry's, and all of our stories, and together, we will help you understand. And like I said, we will bring you up to this point where we are now. You will understand everything and your own part in it all will become clear.

"Now first, you must understand that this whole area is very sensitive. When I say this area, I mean the land here. It is an old area and is very strong with the presence of people like us. People who have died in very emotional circumstances. Now please Andrew, time is against us; will you listen to us?"

Again, Andrew nodded. He looked directly at Emily's face as she took his head in her hands. She stared directly into his eyes. "Okay, Andrew, this is how it will be. I will open your mind for you so that you may hear the voice. You shall hear and know all the voice tells you, and know His words for the truth. It is much quicker than speech; now empty your mind and receive Him."

Henry lay on the hard floor; his mind had gone blank. He could no longer feel the pressure on him or the cold, but he could hear the lord talking. "You did this. You brought this on us all," he heard him say. "I found your journal and I know what filthy disgusting acts that you committed with our last splitter and what fruit came forth from that whoring, you damned disgusting woman. Maybe now you can go to him in his cold unmarked grave behind the stable and warm each other."

Henry did not really understand the words for they were not spoken to him, but unlike himself, they were warm and strangely soothing to him. He was dead, this much he understood. He got to his feet and followed the lord into the house.

He found his dear friend Molly and would watch her at play with her toys. He was there and watched silently when Edward came and moved her things, hiding them from her. Henry did not like Edward. He did not like him near her. Molly was his friend and Henry decided that he would protect her. It was an instinctive thing for Henry.

He just knew that Edward was a threat. Edward posed danger and meant harm towards his little friend. He did not know why, but Henry knew that he himself was strong. His very presence so far was enough to keep Edward at bay and away from her. So, Henry stayed close by Molly's side at all times.

Sometimes, Molly seemed to sense Henry near and knew he was there with her. She seemed to take comfort from this and would talk and sing to him just like she used to. Molly was strong for her age and when finally Henry visibly appeared before her, she looked up at him and smiled lovingly at her dear friend.

Henry would play with Molly and show her the stumps where his hands used to be. She did not mind this; she enjoyed her time with Henry and made him show her all the time. Until one day, she was caught playing by Lord Castleleigh and he forced her to send Henry away. Being the kind and gentle soul he was, Henry could not resist, and when Molly told him to go, he had no choice.

It was then that Edward saw his opportunity; he returned to seek his revenge. Henry was shocked by Edward's new-found strength and power. Edward killed Molly and the lord. He utterly destroyed them and mutilated their still warm bodies. He stole the lord's hands and Molly's head, whilst Henry watched, distraught and impotent to act against him.

Because of her command, Henry was powerless to intervene and could only return to be with them once they were dead. Edward turned to face Henry. "I go now, but be warned. When I return, I will be all powerful. None shall stand before my might, and any who try shall be swept aside. He who was cast out has come to me, he is in me. Now, and forever. We will meet again, Henry." Edward left Henry alone with the mutilated, handless body of his former master and the decapitated body of his beautiful, young and special friend.

Henry sat with the bodies, sobbing and waiting until they rose. It was at this point that Henry heard the voice speak to him for the first time. It told Henry that He had been watching him. The voice explained that Molly, being a child, was not permitted to stay, and so she had to go on to the next plane.

Lord Castleleigh was given the choice to stay with and help Henry or to go with Molly. The lord wanted nothing to do with Henry and therefore chose to go, leaving Henry alone once more.

The voice spoke to Henry. It told him of the dark forces gathering, of how they sought to open the veil to the world of the living. It told him that he would be the champion. That he must stay and defend this realm from the evil. The voice told Henry that one day, he would be needed and that he must offer his protection to those who needed it. So Henry stayed, alone. For years, he wandered the lands as the voice had commanded him, watching for the dark forces. The advent of Constance spelled a deep trouble, but after her death, Henry could relax a little. She could have spelt disaster for all he fought for, she still could, one day.

As the years rolled by, the familiar changed, new faces came and went. Henry watched over them all, he followed the wishes of the voice. Henry protected and guided souls from one plane to the next. He answered the prayers of the living. Henry protected the innocent and watched over loved ones.

Finally, after many years, Henry sensed a powerful and evil force had come. He could feel the evil. Henry moved quickly to where he perceived the evil was. He came upon the devastated Julia as she stood by her sister's mutilated corpse. Henry was unsure of himself. He wanted to go to her, to save her.

But that was not the voice's will. Freewill was given to all, and so Henry had no choice as he watched and listened and cried as Julia took her own life.

"You may have killed her in this life, but I killed you. I own your spirit now. I will follow you into the next life and all others and will always be there to guard my sweet sister from you. I will pursue you for the rest of time if I must, killing you over and over again."

Henry watched with great sadness as Julia plunged the carving knife deep into her own heart and collapsed down upon William. Henry instinctively knew that, even with her great sin, Julia was to become an ally and, through her actions, would have power over this evil man, something that would help them both. Henry was not the simple man he once had been; he had learnt much from the teachings of the voice.

William clambered to his feet. He looked down at his own and Julia's dead bodies. He took one look at Henry, turned and fled. Henry had done nothing to try and stop William and in doing so, let him escape. Henry knew that he should have stopped William, but his gentle soul would not let him. His main concern was for the twin sisters lying dead upon the cold, hard floor. Henry would not see William again for many years.

Henry waited for Julia; she rose shortly after. She ignored Henry and went to the mutilated body of her sister Emily. Emily 'awoke', screaming. The pain and suffering she had endured in life was still strong within her. It took many hours for Julia to calm Emily. It was then that they noticed Henry was still with them. He had been patient; he knew they would need the guidance and so waited. It was then the voice came once more.

"Emily, the choice is yours. You may come with me to a safer, better place on the other side. But I would ask this of you. The man who killed you is evil. He has killed before and will kill again. You have the chance to stay with Henry, to protect those who cannot protect themselves. People like you were. I will not force or command you, for it is your decision alone to make.

"Julia, you, however, must stay. I cannot allow you to cross whilst the essence of William exists. You made the vow to stop him and therefore, I will hold you to it. You must remain here. You took your own life and are therefore not permitted to go, yet. You are not alone; Henry will be with you. There will come a time when you are needed to protect the living from the coming evil.

"If you heed my will, you may yet gain redemption and entrance to my realm. You must help prevent their forces from destroying and controlling all. They will try to rise and gain power; it will be for you to stop them from achieving this. You shall be not only my champions but my will, when you confront them."

Julia looked to Henry and nodded. Emily embraced her sister. She was not a religious person like her husband, until now. Emily claimed that no message from the lord could be clearer and swore to stay and help protect those who needed their help.

Henry did not know much, and understood even less, of the gods or The God, but he believed in the voice that he heard and served faithfully.

Together, Henry, Julia and Emily roamed. They watched for the return of William and the coming of the prophesied evil forces. They watched over the living. Nothing of consequence happened for years upon years until the arrival of the mass murderer, James Pembleton.

Henry, Julia and Emily were not witness when James arrived in their plane of existence. They were ignorant of his murders and of his many victims. They were not privy to all knowledge and so they did not know him. They did become very aware of him, however, when they felt his strong evil presence among them.

They tried to find him but when they arrived, too late, all they found was the empty shell of a body that had once belonged to James Pembleton.

The voice returned to them, something that had not happened for over a hundred years.

"It is coming. You are too late, and now William has gained a very powerful ally in his quest. Together, they are strong and if they remain united in their cause, they will rival your powers. If they are allowed to continue, they will recruit others to their cause and succeed in pulling down the veil between the worlds of the living and the dead. The veil that I fashioned, and have so long sought to safeguard. They will have power over the living and will be unstoppable. If this happens, they will destroy you three easily."

The voice told them of the meeting between William and James.

You killed me, you fuckin killed me, was the last conscious thought to ever cross the living mind of the mass murderer known as James Pembleton.

I am not dead, you stupid bitch, you didn't finish me, were the very first thoughts ever to cross his dead mind.

"Hello, James."

James jumped to his feet as he saw William immaculately dressed, stood in the building site in front of him.

"Who the fuck are you? Where's the bitch gone?"

"Such language, I find this new world is so vulgar," William said, smiling at James. "You, my friend, are dead. That 'bitch' killed you. You have been laying here for some time now, but it is time we left. He has sent me to retrieve you and we do not want to be found here when they arrive."

"Dead? Yes, yes, I am. But I asked you a question, now tell me who the fuck are you?"

"I, James, am your future. If you want to stay here and let them come for you, fine; you shall have neither future nor vengeance. You shall be destroyed and forgotten. But if you want to join with me now, together we can find the real power so we may kill again. Then come with me to him now."

James did not have to think; a chance to kill once more overrode any other questions he had. William and James left the area and fled to the safety of him before anyone could find them. William told James all about their powers and how, together, they could become powerful enough to invade the living world. How they would be able to kill and torture at their pleasure. They need only find a vessel sensitive enough from the living world to help them. They disappeared for a few more years, all the time gaining strength and learning, whilst planning their return according to his instructions.

All was quiet until the event of Catherine and Oliver's arrival.

Catherine was ill, she had what is known as post-natal depression and her mind was a very fragile thing. The house that they lived in was built very close to the grounds that Lord Castleleigh's house stood, hundreds of years before. The whole area was extremely ripe with energy. Catherine was on medication for her condition but her mind was easily accessible for certain powers.

William sensed Catherine's weakened mind, he saw Catherine as the vessel he needed and jumped the gun somewhat; he saw the weak-willed woman as their chance to gain access and finally open the veil. He entered her mind, mixing her brain more and more until she barely even knew her own name.

There were days when Henry managed to fight through Catherine's confusion and get close to her. On those days, William's grip would slip, but when Henry was absent, William was free once again to twist her mind. With all the conflicted feelings that invaded her fragile mind, Catherine did not understand what she was doing.

In a moment of madness, she killed her own children, thinking they were the ones responsible and that her actions would free her. Oliver found his wife and realised what she had done to his children. By this time, William knew she would not be the one to help him and had abandoned her, leaving Catherine's living mind utterly destroyed.

In his grief, Oliver killed his wife. He put his family together and burnt them all, himself included. Oliver's only regret of this action was that he never quite managed to return to them for their final embrace. In death though, Catherine was finally released.

"Oliver, Oliver, I…I'm so sorry. My darlings, I never would have."

Catherine broke down in tears of devastation as Oliver rose and came to her. He lay down with his family, finally in death was he able to hug his wife and children once more.

"Don't cry, Mummy, it's all okay now," Peter said to his mother as he hugged her fiercely.

The voice returned.

"It is a sad day, one full of much sorrow, but your grief is not yet over. Your children are not only innocents, but they are not to be subject to this evil any further. They must come with me to the beyond, but not you. You two must stay.

Catherine, your father is waiting and will care for Peter and Stacey until your task is complete. If you follow my will, then your actions here, intentional or not, may be forgiven."

Fresh tears cascaded down both Catherine and Oliver's faces as they realised that their children were going to be taken from them again. Before anyone could speak, Peter and Stacey were gone.

Catherine first saw it as her lord punishing her for her sins. But she understood her actions and knew that her children were now in a better place.

Henry, Julia and Emily now stood in their place. The voice continued.

"Catherine, it was William who destroyed your mind and forced all of this. I offer you now a chance of redemption and self-forgiveness. The chance for you to follow me in the attempt to destroy this evil that plagues upon the innocent. Henry, you were warned they would try this. It is fortunate for everyone that they failed this time or everything would now be lost.

"Catherine and Oliver will now aid you in stopping the evil. They too have lost much because of it. The love they carry for that which they have lost will make them strong for what you must do. It will not be long.

"James will soon find them a willing and living participant who will bring others. They will die and the veil will be opened; that cannot be prevented now. It has been a long time in coming but it is nearly here. He who I cast out so long ago is aiding them. He has hidden himself well from me. I have only recently become aware of this.

"I have not though, yet discovered the guise he now wears. Your only hope now lies with Sarah."

"Wait," Julia said, "who is Sarah? How shall we find her?"

"You must watch for William and James. Sarah will not come alone. Remember, Julia, you have the power over William. You have stopped him before and you must stop him again."

The five of them searched desperately for signs of William and James; finally, they found them. They could not act until James was absent and William was on his own and of course, the foreseen arrival of Sarah.

Henry and the others observed, but could only sit powerless as William and James found a family to draw strength from. They fed well upon the fears of those living souls. William would show himself, but hideously deformed, to the older woman through her mirror. He loved to hear her screams and relished basking in her fear.

James would fill a bath with his victims' blood and once tried to drown and kill the woman. He was not strong enough alone, and so failed in his attempt.

William came very close to successfully killing the girl. She was weak and let him in.

Henry, acting for the first time against the voice's wishes, refused to sit still any longer. In an act of defiance, Henry intervened and stopped William. He remained there in that place, as guard to watch over the girl.

In his weakened and angered state, William attempted to murder the man who lived there, but this time, Julia was ready and stopped him again. She held him, breaking their plans. Knowing that all was lost and they could not win, James fled; he went in search of the one who would help them. He found Paul.

Paul was a powerful psychic medium. He charged huge amounts of money to those who wanted to speak to loved ones who had died. He was sensitive but most of the time, he had to fake his powers, as contact between the living and dead worlds was almost impossible. Unless of course, the dead were powerful enough to act on the contact Paul attempted. James was one such and he was strong; he found Paul and saw him as the answer to opening the veil.

Paul, you are the one.

Paul was startled but it was not the first time he had spoken to someone from the other side.

"Who are you?"

My name is James, and I need your help.

"What do you need?"

With your help, I can cross over once more and carry on my work in the living world.

James told Paul all about himself and William. He explained how, with his help, they would open the veil. He said he could make Paul a god amongst men. How, if they helped one another, they could destroy the veil separating the worlds.

Paul in his thirst for power, sick of being the target of sceptics and non-believers, agreed to help. He joined with the people who would soon visit the home that William was now trapped in. Together, they would bring the prophecy to fruition. James stayed at Paul's side as everything finally began to take shape and come together.

Finally, after all those long years, the time had come, and it started. Henry and Julia's failure to obey the voice could have proven disastrous to everyone.

He had a plan, one that would have simultaneously destroyed the evil and saved all. That plan, because of Henry and Julia, and their lack of patience, was now gone.

Sarah and Andrew entered the property, they were naïve in their approach and William actually laughed at them while they tried to make contact. In his struggle with Julia, he even managed to move the table. Julia still controlled him and she stopped him from interacting with them further.

With William still trapped, she made a fatal error. Julia left him unguarded and she used her valuable energies in contacting and trying to warn Andrew off. Knowing what was coming, and with Henry occupied elsewhere, Julia was desperate. But then Paul arrived, and with him, James.

Julia was attacked and quickly subdued, made powerless and trapped by James and a now free William. The newcomers were oblivious to all of this. She was neutralised. This left William free once more as Paul led the newcomers to their doom and his freedom.

The voice's plan had fallen apart and failed. Hundreds of years in the planning and now it was gone. They had briefly lost faith and not heeded His will. The evil was coming, now, and no one could see it.

"There is still hope. Have faith, Andrew, and help them."

Andrew jumped to his feet away from Emily, his understanding of what was happening complete. It was clear to him that they had all been played for fools by Paul right from the beginning.

"Bastard, I'll fucking kill him," Andrew shouted furiously. Emily stood and held Andrew by his trembling shoulders. He looked up at her, their eyes met.

"Andrew, please, you must listen to me. Yes, it is true that Paul is in part responsible for some of this. But you must understand, from all you have seen, that the events happening now were put into motion hundreds of years ago. If it was not Paul they used, it would have been another. He is in some ways as much a pawn and innocent as you are. He was destined to aid the evil just as you have been destined to die here for many years."

"I don't give a damn shit about me," he said angrily. "I do not give a damn about your voice, or…or your god, or whatever the hell that was. But I do give a damn about my sister who is outside this place with my best friend, and his girlfriend is trapped upstairs with those…those…"

"It is okay, Andrew, my sister is in danger too, and although we are dead, it is very possible for us to die again. It is hard to explain. We are in a great many ways like the living; cut us and we will bleed. We are the same as them, just existing on a different plane.

"Our difference is that if we die then it is over, there is no possibility of us passing on. We will just cease to be. As you were told, Andrew, if you die, two things can happen. You will either move on to your next existence on the other side, or you become like us, with work to do.

"Whilst we exist in this place still, our energies are beyond His power. Therefore, should we die, then it is over. Our energies will disperse and we are no more. Our reward for staying here and being successful in what He commands is to join with Him for all time in the next step of our existence.

"So you see, Andrew, in a way, we have more to lose than your friends do. We will get no second chance if we die this day. We must have faith. We must work together, to save the others and prevent this from happening. We will put trust in you, leave it for you to try and contact your sister; after all, out of everyone, your connection with her will be the strongest.

"You must convince her and Tom to leave; remember, Andrew, that is your only job. Please heed me, you have not been one of us long and so you are not strong, you must not under any circumstances confront the others, they will easily and without conscience kill you.

"Oliver will go and join Henry. Together, I hope they may be strong enough to get Sarah out. I will confront William whilst Catherine distracts James. Hopefully, we can survive long enough that I will be able to attempt to rescue Julia. Remember, this room is the only place that belongs solely to us. It is the one safe place we have that they cannot enter.

"They need an invitation from the living to enter here, and that is something they will never have. You will be safe here. If all goes well, Henry and Julia will be with us again, we may hear His voice once more and exert His will. If not, then all is already lost. Please do not give up; I never will. Good luck, my dear friends."

Paul ran from the house; he crossed the lawn and threw open the car door. He looked from one face to the other as he fought to catch his breath. Tom sensed trouble as he noticed the blood on Paul's hand and arm. He was out of the car in a split second. He grabbed Paul by the collar, pushing over and pinning him to the bonnet as Jessica hurriedly climbed out after them.

"What's going on in there, Paul? Whose blood is that? Why didn't we see anything on the cameras? Tell me, damn you," Tom screamed into Paul's terrified and suddenly pale face.

Paul was great at calm arguments and he was great with the dead, but he detested physical violence. Especially when that violence was aimed towards him.

"Tom, please, it's Sarah, she's hurt," he whimpered.

"What? Where? Tell me now," Tom said, calmer now. A hint of fear became abundantly clear in his voice.

"Inside; come, I'll show you. She's upstairs, she called out and something flew across the room and hit her. She's alive but unconscious. Now what are you going to do, Tom?" He sneered. "Beat me up for trying to help your girlfriend or are you coming in to help her?"

Tom released his hold and stepped back. "I'm sorry, Paul, I didn't mean to. I just saw the blood and panicked. Please, lead the way."

Paul straightened himself up and smoothed out his jacket. He started off across the lawn once more, but this time with Tom following close behind.

Tom paused at the door long enough to call back to Jessica. "Stay put, Jess, we won't be long."

Jessica was left standing alone, staring at Tom's back as he disappeared with Paul into the house. The front door slammed shut behind them.

Andrew looked at his sister, realising that he had arrived too late to save his best friend Tom, but at least his sister was still safe.

"Stay here, my arse," Jessica muttered to herself. "She's my friend too." And she took off across the lawn towards the house.

Jess, no. Come back. Please, you can't go in there, Andrew begged his sister's back as she ran. But Emily had been right. Jessica was not sensitive and he was just not strong enough yet. Andrew stood powerless and impotent as he watched his best friend and his sister disappear inside the house. Andrew fell to his knees as they vanished from his sight and to their almost certain deaths.

Andrew knelt for some time before he understood what it was that he had to do. He could not obey Emily's wishes. He had to try and save his sister. The higher power be damned.

Chapter 13
2012 – First and Second Deaths

The door to Alice's room shut quietly but with a firm click. Sarah glanced nervously over towards the door. She quickly realised that Henry most likely was the one responsible for the door shutting. He was probably thinking that he was protecting her. Sarah did indeed feel safe in Henry's large arms, but she knew she couldn't remain in Alice's room if the others needed her. "Henry, we can't stay here. We have to go."

No. We wait. We go soon.

Sarah was confused, why did they have to wait? If Paul was indeed in league with the bad spirits as Henry had suggested, then surely, they should go and warn the others; delaying could solve nothing. But it could worsen things.

Sarah's thoughts were interrupted by the sounds of raised voices. She could not make out what was being said but it sounded to her like an argument. Sarah thought she heard Paul, but she heard no more as the voices abruptly stopped when what sounded to her like something heavy being repeatedly slammed down. There was one final dull thud followed by what sounded like something heavy, a person perhaps, someone falling over? All became quiet until she could make out the sounds of somebody running down the stairs.

Sarah eased from Henry's embrace as she stood and took a small wary step towards the closed door. She stopped in her tracks when she heard a knocking from the other side of the door. Sarah even backed up a couple of steps, walking into the now solid form of Henry, when she heard the dark sinister voice on the other side of the door.

Open up, Henry, your time is up. We want her.

The doorknob began to turn and shake.

Sarah turned around in fright as she felt a huge electric current charge the room and found herself staring at a massive chest. Henry was visible. She could see him as clearly as she could see any other living person. Sarah looked up past his filthy, torn shirt to his thick neck and up to his kindly face. He was not a handsome man, but he radiated a kindness, an aura of power and safety. Sarah looked at his muscular arms and down to the stumps of his wrists that slowly dripped a deep crimson blood down onto the carpet.

Tears filled Sarah's eyes as she looked up at the brave man who was protecting her. "Who…who is it, Henry?" she asked quietly as Henry moved in front of her, placing himself between Sarah and the rattling door.

Bad people, we wait.

The door stopped rattling and Sarah breathed, she hadn't realised that she was holding her breath.

They gone; now, we go.

Henry walked to the door as it swung open, apparently of its own accord before him. Henry looked down. He shook his great head as he turned to Sarah.

Stay with me, you safe. We go where they no hurt you, come.

Sarah followed Henry from the room, she gasped and her hand flew to her chest. She looked down to see a man lying on the floor just outside the room. He had a glowing aura around him. There were thick bruises around his neck where it was clear that he had been strangled to death. Henry looked down at his friend again sadly. The man disappeared leaving no trace of ever having existed.

Oliver is gone now. He gave his second life so we would have time to go. Come, we must hurry to the safe place. Follow Henry.

Sarah followed Henry across the landing and down the stairs. She kept looking around nervously, turning on any light switch she passed. They made it into the sitting room with no incidents or problems.

The room was empty. Sarah sat down on the same armchair she had previously sat on no more than half an hour ago, before they had encountered anything. When there was still doubt that there was anything in the house at all. But to Sarah, it felt more like hours ago.

Sarah stay, Henry finds others. You must not leave here. I will come back for you soon.

Sarah only half listened as she looked up and saw the large form of Henry fade and disappear before her eyes. She stood up, there was absolutely no way was she going to sit around waiting and do nothing whilst her friends' lives were in danger. Hearing a door crash closed, Sarah crossed the room and looked out into the hallway as Tom started to climb the stairs.

Sensing movement, Tom looked and spotted Sarah in the sitting room. Tom looked confused as he backed off the stairs and turned towards her. As he made his way towards her, another figure ran up the stairs behind Tom.

Sarah started to walk towards Tom, relieved to see him there. Sarah's smile and sense of relief was short-lived as everything slowed down around her. A well-dressed gentleman calmly stepped in front of Tom and coolly ran the blade of a large hunting knife deep across his bare throat.

Sarah stopped with her heart in her throat as she watched Tom's blood shoot from his neck and fountain across the room towards where she stood. She sank to her knees, mirroring Tom, the blood flow pulsing. She was helpless and paralysed.

All Sarah could do as Tom held his hands to his spurting neck was watch. She watched as his face changed from confusion to panic to fear. She watched as his face paled and his life's blood flowed over and through his fingers and down his shirt. Sarah watched helplessly as the dark red puddle of blood grew in front of Tom. She watched as he finally collapsed face down onto the carpet and into the scarlet pool of his own blood, and moved no more.

Sarah heard soft laughter from behind Tom.

We grow more powerful as their deaths feed our strength. Soon it will be your time, Sarah.

Sarah looked up at the well-dressed gentleman as he smiled at her and faded away, only to be replaced by a stunned-looking Jessica. She stood in the front doorway, her splayed hands covering her mouth and lower face in horror as she looked down at Tom's body and at the still kneeling person that was her friend, Sarah.

Jessica. The thought ripped through Sarah, it brought her back to some semblance of control over her body. She had to save Jessica. What was it Henry had told her? She was safe in this room. *I'm not in this room anymore, I gotta get back.*

"Jess, quick. Come in here," Sarah cried urgently as she staggered to her feet, backing quickly towards the sitting room.

"Wh...what, Sarah what?" Jessica mumbled as she shook her head and stared from Tom to Sarah and back again, over and over.

Sarah could see Jessica was in shock. She knew they didn't have much time and Jessica was in great danger as long as she remained exposed, out in the hallway. As quick as her numb body allowed, she began to move her feet and slowly went to where Jessica stood frozen. Taking her friend gently by the arm, Sarah pulled Jessica after her and back into the sitting room.

Once there, Sarah sat Jessica down on the sofa. Sarah, in control, ran back and shut the sitting room door. She knew there was nothing that she could do for Tom, but she could still help Jessica. Sarah knelt on the carpet in front of her, holding Jessica's hands in her own.

"Jess, Jess, can you hear me?" Sarah said softly to her friend as Jessica just sat and stared through unblinking eyes at the closed door.

"Jess, bad things are happening here, I don't get it and I don't know what it is. A ghost, Henry, he brought me here. He said I would be safe h—" Sarah was cut off mid-sentence by Jessica's sudden cold and emotionless question.

"Where's Andy?" she whispered.

"I…I don't know. He was upstairs wi—"

"Where is my brother?"

"Jess, please," Sarah said. She did not know what to tell her friend. "He was in…" She looked at Jessica's widening eyes. "What is it, Jess?"

"He's alive," Jessica whispered. She jumped to her feet, nearly knocking Sarah over and shouted, "Holy shit. He's…he's still alive, Sarah."

Sarah looked around behind her to where Jessica was looking. She was expecting to see Andrew stood there after Jessica had been asking about him and then stating, 'he's alive'.

She had not expected to see the sitting room door open again and Tom moving. Both relief and shock flooded her rigid body as she stood and watched Tom slowly climb to his feet. He stood watching them, the barest of smiles flickering across his pale face.

Sarah took a step towards him, wanting so much to feel his warm and loving arms around her once more. She stopped, the warm feeling gone and replaced by a heavy dread in the pit of her stomach when she noticed the well-dressed gentleman was back. He once more stood in the hallway at Tom's side.

Here is a little lesson for you, Sarah. Die when you're dead and you stay dead.

Sarah heard the voice and everything around her slowed to a crawl once more. She watched William draw the long blood-stained blade across Tom's throat once again. She stood in horror as Tom again sank to his knees. There was no blood this time as he looked up at Sarah. Tom's wide eyes met her own as he mouthed the words 'I love you'. He fell face first and was forever lost.

You're mine, my sweet.

Sarah heard the voice somewhere in the numb recesses of her mind, but she did not realise how clear and strong it had sounded. William was growing stronger from all the death. She fell back from it as Jessica pulled on her arm and guided her back to the safety of the sitting room. Jessica kicked the door hard and it slammed shut, blocking out the sight of William. Jessica sat down on the carpet, pulling Sarah down with her. They sat together, rocking gently in each other's arms, sobbing quietly.

"Okay Em, get her and let's get the hell out of here."

Emily nodded as she carefully moved across the attic towards where her unconscious sister lay. Catherine was about to follow Emily when a huge, calloused hand clamped down on her shoulder from behind. She opened her mouth and tried to scream out a warning to Emily but another hand snaked across her mouth, containing the scream and silencing her.

James Pembleton pulled Catherine through the square hatch and down to the floor of the upstairs landing. He threw her onto her back and sat, straddled across her chest, his huge hands finding her throat. His long fingers sought to strangle the very existence from her.

She could feel the heavy weight of the beast on her, she felt as her bones broke, as her throat was crushed and collapsed beneath his hands. She could draw no more breath through her destroyed throat and died beneath his evil hands. Catherine died for the second and final time. Her last thought was for her beautiful children, Peter and Stacey, who she would never get to see or hold again.

Emily crouched over her sister. She cradled Julia lovingly in her arms and called gently to her.

Julia slowly began to stir as Emily saw a dark shadow fall across them.

"William." Emily's voice was small, like a frightened child.

"Hello, my dear, sweet Emily. Shall we make our special love once more?"

Emily froze in terror, memories of what this man had done to her before smashed through her mind, as William pulled her from Julia. She was paralysed with fear. The man who had killed her before, began tearing at her clothes. Emily sensed movement as Julia rose to her feet, her eyes wide with anger and teeth bared as she swiftly advanced and attacked William.

Emily watched as William fell before Julia's wrath. He lay unable to defend himself as she punched his face over and over.

Julia froze mid-swing at the sound of the deep booming voice coming from behind Emily.

"Sweet meat, I never had me sisters before."

"Nor will you now."

Emily didn't know where to look first. She was stunned as Andrew came up behind James, wrapping his arms around the big man's waist, and tackled him to the floor. Andrew screamed at Emily, "Get Julia out of here now, I can't hold him for very long."

Emily pulled Julia to her feet, they backed away from a beaten William and turned, just as James struggled and got free from Andrew. James's face twisted into a mask of pure hatred as he grasped Andrew's head on either side and with his huge deadly hands, viciousiy twisted. There was a look of pure shock and disbelief on Andrew's face and a look of triumph on James'. An audible crack sounded loudly in the attic as Andrew's neck broke and he too died again.

Emily pushed her sister down through the hatch. She was confused to see the blatant fear on Julia's face as their eyes met. Something was wrong. Emily saw the knife blade as it briefly reflected in her sister's eyes. She sensed him behind her and she felt the sharp scratch across her throat.

She raised her hand and touched the hot pumping pain. It was warm and sticky on her fingers. She looked for the last time down at the sister who had loved her across the space of time and death, the sister who had always been there for her.

Emily had to make Julia go before they got her as well, she could not, would not allow these evil men to have her sister. She waved for Julia to go. She tried to speak but the knife had cut deep and had severed her vocal cords. All Emily could hope was that Julia saw her lips say 'go, save them'.

Emily could no longer see her sister. She turned her head and saw Andrew's lifeless eyes staring back at her. She saw James Pembleton's dirty work boot as it came into view and crashed down into her face. Emily Farrow saw and felt no more.

William and James jumped down through the attic hatch in pursuit of Julia. They stopped when they saw the huge form of Henry supporting the woman. William took a brave step towards them.

"It is over, Henry. We have won. They are all dead, yours are all dead. We grow ever more powerful. Give us this one and the living woman below and we will make your death quick. We have the one waiting for us, he will open the veil."

Henry smiled at William and pointed to the bathroom door with his bloody stump.

"You mean the one known as Paul? You are too late, I kill him. We go now."

Henry turned and helped the staggering Julia down the stairs as James and William rushed into the bathroom where the body of Paul lay awkwardly on the floor.

James screamed and cursed. He smashed the mirror of the medicine cabinet and put his foot through the side panel of the bathtub in his anger.

William fell to his knees besides Paul's body and rested his hand upon its chest. William's head snapped up as he felt the steady rise and fall of Paul's chest. He grinned up at the terrifying face full of rage that stared in an animalistic snarl back down at him.

"Henry lied to us in order to escape. He has proved that he does not have the stomach to do what he must to defeat us. He is nothing but a weak and lost fool, my friend."

"What do you mean?"

"Paul lives, he is merely unconscious. Henry did not have the strength to do what he should have. And thanks to him, we will win. We know he has not the gift to kill, whilst our ever-growing strength now allows us to attack the living. When Paul helps us get into their place and we capture the woman, we can kill him. With his energies joined to ours, finally it will be over and we will have it all."

James's anger broke into a thin smile as they waited patiently for Paul to recover and regain consciousness. They had waited a long time for this day. It would not be much longer.

Sarah raised her head from Jessica's shoulder as Henry and Julia walked solemnly into the room. Julia closed the door behind her. They stood before them, solid. To Sarah, they were as real as Jessica was. If they were in this form that allowed them to physically interact with the living, Sarah knew that something big had happened or was happening now.

Sarah stood; Jessica stood with her with and together they faced the newcomers, hand in hand. "Henry, where are the others?" Sarah asked.

Henry, his face drawn and full of sadness, lowered his head. Julia looked directly at Sarah. *I am sorry for your losses.*

Jessica was distraught. She almost spat her words at Julia, "Losses? Fucking losses. Where the hell is my brother? Where's the sick bastard who did that thing to Tom?"

Julia remained calm. *Your brother died bravely, he gave his life to help my sister and he saved me. I am deeply sorry for you, but we cannot afford to fall apart now.*

Julia moved to Jessica and placed her hands on either side of Jessica's head. Jessica visibly relaxed and her face went blank, her eyes stared at nothing as she absorbed everything.

After releasing Jessica, Julia looked deep into Sarah's eyes. She held her hands out. A connection with the living had been made, Julia's voice was strong, they all existed on the same plain. The veil was failing.

"It is nearly here and we must be ready. You must be strong for what is still to come. Sarah, will you stand with us?" Julia asked.

Chapter 14
2012 – The Last

"Are we strong enough now? Is it time?" James asked William impatiently as they stood in the hallway next to the closed door of the sitting room.

William turned his head and listened to a voice; a voice unheard by James. He blinked slowly as he turned his head towards James. "Yes," he whispered. "We are strong enough to physically attack the living, but we may only do so in this place. We must destroy the woman, and only then will the veil fall and we shall become all powerful."

James tried the door, his hand jumped off it like there was an electrical current running through the door handle and he pulled his hand back, hissing. "It is still forbidden for us to enter. We must find a way to lure them out and destroy that lumbering idiot and the bitch Julia. Paul, you must enter their place and bring them out," James said to the pale and silent man behind them.

"Me? How…how the hell do I do that?" he said nervously, looking from James to William and back again.

William took Paul by his nervously shaking shoulders. "You are the living and so may enter. Once you get them out, or us in, we will swiftly deal with them. Trust me, my friend, you will be perfectly safe."

Paul nodded uncertainly, sweat running down his face as his clammy hand closed on the doorknob and twisted.

It all happened so fast that Sarah's mind could hardly keep up. The door burst open as Paul charged through. He looked straight at her and screamed for Sarah to help him, to save him. She stood rooted to the spot, unsure, unable to think or process all of what was happening around her. She hated the man with every fibre of her being, but how could she ignore his cry for help? Sarah just watched helplessly as he barrelled straight passed her and into Jessica, sending both of them crashing to the floor.

Paul recovered first. He stood up and quickly turned to the open door. "I am of the living and I now invite you to come into this place," he shouted breathlessly as he turned his attention back to Jessica. He visibly paled and shrank when he saw that Jessica was on her feet facing him.

The look on Jessica's face was pure hatred, pure savagery. Jessica punched Paul hard. She hit him square on his nose. Sarah watched his nose flatten and explode out beneath Jessica's fist. She was hit in the face by his flying blood when Jessica's fist connected again, this time with Paul's jaw, sending his head flying to the side. Paul fell and fell hard. The side of his head smashed into the corner of the table as he fell. A large pool of blood soon formed around his head as he lay unmoving.

William and James had been invited in by the living. They confidently entered the sitting room together. James, hot-headed, charged and went for Henry whilst William, still wanting his revenge, attacked Julia.

James, even with all of his anger and aggression, was no match for Henry, as the Splitting Man swung his arm at James' head with all of his might and muscle. Henry swung like he was felling a tree and James's body arched backwards through the air to land in a crumpled heap. Henry turned to see Julia fall as William pulled the massive blade from her blood-soaked stomach. Henry rushed to her side as she sank to her knees. "Stop them, Henry, You must stop th..." Julia cried weakly.

As Henry began to rise once more, William with two hands plunged the knife blade as deep as he could into Henry's back. Almost simultaneously, a groggy James struggled to his feet, grabbed and smashed him across the back of his head with a small nest table from beside the armchair.

Henry's huge body collapsed and fell defeated to the floor. Still, Sarah stood frozen, watching the carnage and blood all around her.

William advanced on the shocked Jessica. She was staring down at the dead body of Paul as William smashed her across the face. She fell, hard, her head bouncing off the floor. Her eyes still wide open, but unseeing, she did not move again.

Kill him again, William said.
Are you sure? I mean, I thought –

Do it now, you fool, do it and grow strong.

James fell on Paul, he got busy with his hands as he tightened them around Paul's throat, Paul fought back briefly until James twisted. With the crack of his neck, Paul fell still once more.

From the time Paul had burst into the room until the time he died for the second time, no more than a minute had passed.

I'm the only one still alive, Sarah thought as William and James stalked towards her; their faces wore looks of pure triumph.

"Please," was all Sarah managed to say weakly before James attacked her. She lay on her back, his full weight pressing down on her chest and his fingers tight around her throat. Sarah desperately sucked but could draw no breath. Tears escaped her straining and bulging eyes, sliding down her cheeks. Her vision became blurred as her head pounded with the worst migraine she had ever experienced. Finally, mercifully, everything around Sarah went dark.

James climbed off Sarah's body. William smiled at his friend. "Bring her, it is time."

Sarah slowly regained consciousness. Her head was still pounding as she tried to take in her surroundings. Even with everything that had happened, she managed to appreciate the irony of where she was. She was tied up, arms and legs splayed. She was tied to the bedposts of Alice's bed. Sarah thought how it was not long ago she had lay there safe in Henry's arms, knowing that nothing could harm her whilst she was with him.

A few tears of sorrow escaped her as Sarah remembered that Henry was gone. Tom was gone. Andrew was gone. Jessica was gone. Julia and all the others were gone. Soon, she would be dead and gone too.

Sarah welcomed her death at this point. She knew she was weak for wishing it, weak for wanting it. She was done though. She could neither fight nor take any more. Sarah squeezed her eyes shut tight; a last single tear escaped from its corner. Sarah shuddered as she felt a wet pressure press against her cheek, her eyes flew open. She would have screamed was it not for the gag she realised was stuffed in her mouth. William was there. He was licking her face as he grinned down at her.

"Awake at last," William whispered, leering over her face, his foul breath hot against Sarah's cheek.

"I am so sorry to disturb your sleep, my dear, but needs must."

William was there; he was real and solid. Somehow, as had happened with Julia downstairs, the plains of existence had been merged. His form was whole. His voice was no longer heard as if in the background. Nothing separated them, not death, not the veil. Nothing but half a foot of air separated Sarah from William.

Sarah could not see William as he stepped from her field of vision; she tried to turn her head to follow him but found she couldn't. Her head was somehow restrained as well. She felt a cool breeze caress her chest as her blouse was ripped open. She felt cold steel raise goosebumps all across her hot skin as the knife went between the cups of her bra and her chest, and jerked upwards, cutting.

Sarah wanted to be sick as rough hands grabbed at and pulled the bra away from her naked breasts; the hands lingered on her for far longer than was necessary to simply remove her bra. Sarah could taste the bile stirring in the back of her throat, threatening to rise higher and choke her.

Thankfully, finally, the repulsive, groping hands went away.

What returned was worse.

William's face came back into view above her.

"There, that is better. Please do not think us rude, the removal of clothes was necessary. Don't get me wrong; your body is beautiful but I cannot be allowed to be tempted by the flesh now. You see," he said smiling, "we need to see clearly so I know exactly where to cut."

Sarah's eyes stretched wider than ever, she screamed into the gag. Her whole body was writhing and struggling uselessly against her restraining bonds. The thought of her death was forgotten.

The thought of her lost friends and loved ones was forgotten. Only one terrified thought crossed her mind.

They're gonna cut me up.

"Get on with it. I want to get out there and slaughter me some fresh fuckin bitches." Sarah could hear James's gruff voice off to the side and William behind.

"Patience now, my friend, we are nearly there," William said to him quietly.

"Are you sure we can still do this without Paul?"

William looked over his shoulder at James. "Yes, my friend, trust me. That idiot Paul's death added to our power. I can now perform what needs doing to this woman. And I do so with great pleasure. Now stand back whilst I cut and carve out our freedom and future." With knife in hand, William leant in towards Sarah's prone and vulnerable body.

Sarah's teeth clenched down hard against her gag, her body broke out in a freezing sweat as she struggled with every ounce of strength she possessed, with every fibre of her being. Sarah's fists clenched as she tugged against the ropes, arms shaking with the strain.

In her legs, she felt the beginning of cramp as she tugged with the last of her fleeting strength. All the great effort Sarah expended, but it was not enough, she collapsed down, her breath coming in ragged gasps, defeated. Sarah's strength was spent. Her will was broken and gone. She lay still, as she was forced to, and finally accepted her fate.

Sarah did not struggle or flinch as the cold blade edge flattened her nipple and slid slowly down the curve of her breast. Sarah distantly felt the cold sharp tip of the knife as William put it between her breasts. She felt the sharp sting and the warmth of her own blood trickle down her side as the knife pierced her skin.

Sarah felt the definite dragging bite as William began to draw the blade and cut slowly down her body and towards her stomach.

"Stay."

Henry gently placed a restraining stump on Jessica's shoulder. She slumped back down on the sofa where Henry had carefully placed her body upon discovering that she still lived.

Henry was in great pain, more pain than he had ever experienced in life. He felt a deep burning on his back where William's blade had been. He could feel the blood still leaking from his wound. His head felt ready to explode from where the small table James had swung had hit him. His face was streaked with his own blood.

But Henry would not, could not stop now. The threat was real and Henry was still needed. He had made mistakes along the way, but he was still the voice's will. Sarah was still alive and she needed him. He could, and must still try to stop the evil before all was lost. How Henry needed to hear the voice again, he needed its guidance. But the voice was silent.

Henry walked slowly and painfully from the room, he leant heavily on the banister for support as he began to climb the stairs. He knew where William and James held Sarah. The same room he had spent much time in and guarded before

Sarah and the others had shown up. Sarah had not long ago felt safe there with him; he would make sure that she would feel that way again.

Henry stopped in front of the door to Alice's room. He took a step back, raised his left leg and kicked with all of his strength. The door burst open, literally exploding from its hinges as Henry strode into the room. Anger flared through him at what he witnessed.

William stayed with his back to Henry, but James turned and faced Henry.

James rushed towards Henry. He smashed into him knocking the giant of a man back. Henry's back hit the wall, his legs buckled and he slid to the floor. Struggling to rise, James punched Henry in the face several times until Henry fell again. James laughed at the weakened Henry. Grabbing his head and forcing Henry to face him, he taunted him, begged him to get up and fight. James let go of his head, he kicked out, foot connecting with jaw and down Henry went again.

On stumps and knees, Henry struggled up. As James advanced once more, Henry managed to get his arms up and feebly push him back, giving himself a moment to regroup, to think. Henry knew he couldn't win; he had no chance against James. Looking beyond James, he could see the knife in William's hand as he cut into Sarah. He knew he needed help; there was only one being he knew with the power that could help him.

Henry looked down at his right stump. He closed his eyes in a silent prayer to the voice. As he opened his eyes again, Henry looked at his hand and relished the feeling he had not felt in countless years. He felt blessed as the blood rushed through his new fingers. He smiled at James as he flexed his new fingers, his fist clenching and unclenching.

James's mouth fell open in shock as he stared in disbelief at Henry. He took a fearful step back as he saw what Henry's new hand now held in its grasp.

Henry raised his hand. The huge wood axe he wielded, too heavy by far for many, but almost weightless in the powerful hand of the Splitting Man. Henry swung and brought the axe head crashing down on top of James's skull. The axe caved his skull in as it tore through him like a hot knife through butter. James's head split in two.

The downward thrust continued. Henry carved straight down through his neck and carried on down through his torso towards James's stomach before the momentum stopped. Henry heaved his axe free, pulling intestines and other internal organs slopping out with it. Henry stood still and watched James.

James just stood for a minute. His ruined face, a blank mask of gore as blood began to seep from his long wound and soon turned into a red geyser. Half his head fell to one side whilst the remaining half fell to the other side. His neck followed suit along with his torso. James literally fell apart. The few remaining internal organs he had left spilled and splashed from his split body and fell into the deepening pool of blood and guts at his feet.

James Pembleton fell to his knees, blood splashing from the impact, his body settled like a giant 'V', his arms bent, his elbows touching the floor either side of his body supporting him like a tripod. James's elbows were all that prevented him from falling further and splitting apart completely.

Henry advanced upon William. He looked past him to the body on the bed. He saw an unmoving Sarah, tied down, sweaty and bloody. An anger, more intense than any he had ever felt, stirred inside Henry as he prayed to the now silent voice that he was not too late.

The knife slowly travelled from between her breasts, down to her stomach. Sarah felt the intense hot burn of the slicing blade, but she was too far gone to care anymore.

As William began cutting across from one side of her to the other just beneath her breasts, Sarah had heard a vague crashing from across the room. She cared not what the noise was. She just wanted to die and for this to be over.

Sarah closed her eyes for what she thought the last time.

A heavy pressure hit down upon Sarah's stomach. *This is it. He just stabbed me with the knife,* Sarah thought. She could feel the blood, and lots of it, spread out across her body and run down her sides to soak into the bed beneath her. *How long,* she wondered, *how long now till I die?*

Sarah was confused. With all of the blood she felt across her body and soaking into the sheets all around her, she wondered why it didn't hurt more. *Should I not be screaming in pain? I should be cold or something.* Confused thoughts flew through Sarah's mind at a million miles an hour.

Sarah felt her head move freely for the first time since her ordeal had started. The restraints holding her had been removed. Sarah's arms moved by themselves and her legs too, both her arms and legs moved to her sides. She was no longer tied up, that much Sarah knew.

Or maybe I'm really dead and this is how it feels to leave my body.

Something was wrong about it all. Sarah knew somehow, something had happened to change her situation. Sarah opened her eyes.

Sarah didn't understand what was happening as she looked up into the kindly and rugged face of Henry. He smiled down at her.

"Sarah safe now. Bad men gone."

Sarah slowly and painfully sat up on the bed. She felt the blood run down and pour from her. *How could I have possibly lost so much blood and still live,* she thought. *Because I am dead. Because I have come back like Henry and the others. But why does it still hurt?*

Looking over the side of the bed, Sarah got her answer. William…well, most of him anyway…lay on the floor, his head had come to a stop some further distance away. It was his blood hitting her that she had felt before.

I'm not dead.

Henry's voice brought Sarah back from her thoughts. "You and Jessica must go now. Henry must burn this place."

Henry turned and vanished into the air as Sarah painfully got up. Realising her nakedness, she removed the last cut rags of her blouse.

Standing in front of the mirror, Sarah used the remains of the blouse to wipe the worst of the blood from her body. Sarah looked at herself in the mirror. The bleeding had nearly stopped, but she could clearly see the cut where it ran down from between her breasts to her stomach. She could also see the thin cut that ran across her chest, just below her breasts.

Sarah gasped in surprise as Henry appeared in the mirror behind her. She turned around to face him.

"Close eyes, Sarah."

Sarah felt safer with Henry than with anyone else she had ever known before. Without question, she obeyed his voice and closed her eyes.

A warm, comforting sensation touched her. Sarah felt the firm pressure of one of Henry's fingers between her breasts. It was not in any way sexual, but it was beyond intimate. Henry's finger ran the length of the cut. Sarah could feel her cuts closing and healing as Henry's hand touched her. When the hand went away, Sarah was left feeling warm and calm.

Sarah opened her eyes. Henry was gone, so too were her cuts. She squinted to look at herself, but could only make out a thin pink cross on her body. Sarah ran her own hands over where the cuts were. All Sarah could feel was a slight ridge where they had been.

Sarah moved. She rummaged through Alice's chest of drawers in search of something to wear. She found a pink T-shirt, too small but obviously much better than wearing nothing, she decided. Putting the tight shirt on, Sarah walked out of the room. She walked past the mess that was James's split body, she spat on him as she went. Her voice hissed through clenched teeth. "No less than you fucking deserve, you sick bastard." her voice softened as she smiled. "Thank you, Henry, thank you." She walked through the door and down the stairs to where Jessica sat waiting for her on the sofa.

Jessica jumped up and into Sarah's arms at seeing her. "Sarah, thank god. Are you okay?" she said, crying into her friend's hair as they hugged. "We have to go, Henry told me once he freed you, we must get out fast and run."

Sarah stood away from Jessica; she was exhausted but tried desperately to focus on Jessica's words.

"He's gonna burn the place, isn't he?"

"Yeah," Jessica said. "He said something about removing all the evidence. He said we can't be here."

The tears came, they overflowed Sarah's eyes and spilt in a torrent down her face; she couldn't wipe them away fast enough. "But, Jess, what about Tom? What about Andrew? We…we can't just leave them here."

Jessica's face grew hard at Sarah's words. "I saw lots of things from Julia. And I saw signs, warnings of many more terrifying things to come whilst I was unconscious. It sounds strange, I know, but I heard this voice telling me stuff. I will tell you about it properly later. But for now, we must go."

Jessica took Sarah by the hand. She led her out of the house and down to the waiting car. Jessica helped Sarah in and made sure she was safely strapped in before closing the car door. Jessica pulled all of the cables clear from the car and shut the back doors; she turned back to face the house one last time.

Henry was stood silently, watching them from the open doorway as thick black smoke began to billow out from the door behind him and every window. Henry raised his left arm to Jessica, urging her to take Sarah to safety and go.

"See you soon, Henry," Jessica said sadly as she smiled towards where Henry had stood.

He was gone. Jessica walked around the car. She opened her door and climbed into the driver's seat. She slammed the door and turned the key in the ignition. Turning the headlights on and selecting first gear, Jessica turned the car around and drove away.

Nothing was said between the two women as Jessica drove down the road. Both of them were lost in their own thoughts of what had happened to them and what they had lost that night.

Jessica was trying to decide when and how she was going to tell Sarah what the voice had told her.

As the car drove away down the street, neither Sarah nor Jessica looked back as the house and garden behind them became a raging inferno, collapsing down upon and consuming itself as it was utterly destroyed.

James 2:14-27

What good is it, my brothers, if a man claims to have faith but has no deeds? Can such faith save him? Faith by itself, if it is not accompanied by action, is dead.

Epilogue

Splitting Man

"Was that the best your so-called champions could do? I almost pity them for their weak and foolish belief in you to guide them. My two destroyed them with no effort. Just think what I will do to any that you send against me."

"They are noble and caring souls. Your evil will never destroy them."

"You are a foolish old being, gone are the days when I feared of your wrath. You may have cast me out once, and for that, I now thank you. But now I warn you, beware, for I come for you. Your precious veil is all but destroyed, I will destroy these souls and then I will destroy you."

"Whilst they still have faith and follow my will, you cannot win. I know your name and I know your guise now. Henry knows of what you did to his most precious friend many years ago. He is not my only champion, but he is enough."

"We will see, old one, we will see how far faith goes when the dead spill out and teem upon the earth. I will watch their faith in you crumble and I shall laugh. I will watch all of your houses around the earth fall apart, and finally, when you have lost all, I will watch the Almighty collapse. I shall stomp you beneath my boot and kick your dust to the four winds."

"We will stop you. Faith is stronger than any fear."

"Keep thinking that, my old fool. You keep thinking whilst I come for everything. The time is almost here, she who is of my blood will aid me and we will be unstoppable. I will show you what real power is. Even your faith will crumble, this is the last of your time. I will see you upon the field of battle soon. I will see you and all who follow you gone."

Henry walked slowly away from the smouldering remains of the house that had been witness to so much sadness and tragedy.

He was sad to have lost his dear friends, friends that had been his family for countless years. But the thought of having finally stopped the evil after all of those years was enough to cheer him slightly. That plus, of course, the fact that now it was finished. His task, his purpose for remaining on in the world was complete. Henry wished that he may be allowed to pass over, see and be with his dear friend Molly once more. Molly, who had been Henry's anchor and his heart. Molly, who, through the long years, had never been far from Henry's thoughts.

The thought of her buoyed him up as he walked. Henry was not sure where he was going or how to get there. His axe was slung across his back, Henry just walked.

The voice returned to Henry.

"Henry, you did well but I have terrible news for you."

Henry turned in a circle, looking all around as he tried to find the location of the disembodied voice.

"We stopped evil, we won. Henry made safe."

"No, Henry, we failed. You did not stop the evil. We were all fooled by his trickery. You merely stopped the evil's distraction. Even as we talk, she is raised from the dead."

Henry did not understand the words he was hearing, he had just lost many good friends and he was being told what? That everything he had done and fought for had been for nothing?

"No, we did. Julia, Emily, Oliver and Catherine die, and Sarah's friends too. But Henry stopped them."

"No, Henry. These you stopped were indeed an evil upon the world, but they were not the evil. The true evil tricked us all. He made us think these were the ones whilst he hid away in secret and grew strong."

"Who is it?" Henry's voice grew strained and weak.

"Henry, listen to me, there are others who can help. One such is Lucy, and she has a very difficult decision to make. She must choose her path to us. It will be full of pain and she will suffer greatly before the time of her choice. You must go to her, Henry, you must help guide her. Now, as to who he is, search your mind, Henry, the answer you seek is there."

Henry was not a clever man, but somehow, he knew. The images flashed like a kaleidoscope through his mind. He remembered the words. 'He who was cast out has come to me, he is in me. Now, and forever. We will meet again, Henry.'

Henry remembered his beautiful little friend who he once played and sang songs with, he remembered the blood.

"Yes, Henry, it is him. You have stopped him once, Henry, many years ago when he was weak. But he has grown strong over the centuries, Henry. He has been killing for many years. A great number have fallen to him. He is now more powerful than any other I have ever encountered. He is, I fear, grown more powerful than me. And he is coming now. There will be, I fear, no stopping the evil that resides within Edward this time. He means to take the world and shape it into his own image that is death. Heed my words, Henry, The Splitting Man is coming."

eyeball 2012

Henry and James